Warning:

This book is truly bi-polar.

Robot God / Hybrid Brain

and other mind-bending stories

by Matt Payne

Cover art by Martin MacPherson

Edited by Cameron Pierce, Bradley Sands, and Garrett Cook

http://www.pattmayne.com

http://martinmacpherson.tumblr.com/

Tracklist:

-Warning

Flocking Shrouds..............................3
Real Hector...................................15
Robot God / Hybrid Brain...............37
Trolling Racoons............................61
Banana Egg Dihydroxybenzene...........65
War as a Machine.............................71
Rakikomaly...79
Art Lover..89
Ghost Dog Writer..................................101
Demon Numbers.............................113

3

The Flocking Shrouds

4

A hooded figure glided down the dark street in a brown robe, only a silhouette visible between the shadows. The cracked streets were empty and the deteriorating low-income housing was silent. Yet the hooded traveller made no footstep-noises, and moved with a confident speed through the lonely neighbourhood.

His path was dark and obscure but his destination was clear. He had an invitation. An intriguing invitation which opened the door to strange questions. "*I am not the only one?*" he wondered. "*There is another like me?*"

He came to the outskirts of downtown and found the shop where the letter said to meet. The sign above the wooden door said, "*Medieval Medical Supplies. For all your Medieval Medical Needs.*" The two glass windows showed off their wares, equipment that looked like torture devices. The door was unlocked. The hooded figure blew in like a windblown rag.

All was silent and dim. Tables and glass cases throughout the room displayed drills, saws, clamps, and instruments of brutal healing. Jagged things for cutting, and straps for holding down the benefactor. The visitor stood in the middle of it all, listening for sounds, looking for the one who had invited him here. His thick brown robes seemed to ripple with life even as he stood still. "Hello," he said. His voice emanated from every part of his being. "Why did you invite me here?"

There was a flash of steel as three scalpels

shot out from a hidden corner of the room. The blades whipped through the air and plunged into the hooded figure's torso... and just as quickly they burst out through his back to slam into a wooden display case.

There was no blood. Just some scraps of torn cloth. The hooded robe collapsed as if there had been no body inside. The brown scraps slithered away across the floor, melting into the dark shadows of the unlit room.

The only light was from the street outside, and a digital clock on the counter at the rear. A large sheet of blue cloth floated up from behind a display case, blocking out half the street-light. There was a pattern on it sewn in white thread, a mandala, and it looked like a decorative rug. It trembled and spoke, “I see you are like me! Living cloth! I have either finally found a friend, or my one worthy nemesis!”

The brown cloth emerged from his hiding place, rising up again into the shape of a hooded human. “Was it you who invited me here?”

The blue rug stayed flattened out, floating above a tray of bone-saws. “No. Perhaps we were both invited here by the same person... maybe a third cloth-being! But tell me, why do you maintain your human form here, when there are no humans around to fool?”

The brown cloth shrugged ghost-shoulders and said, “This is the form I prefer.”

“I prefer freedom! I prefer spontaneity, nonconformity, adapting my shape to every situation. I want a new shape every moment, always changing instead of seeking the comfort of a geometrical familiarity. I was thinking about killing you, but maybe now I will wait until our host arrives!"

The two cloths noticed movement from an air-vent at the back of the room. The panel opened and black fabric oozed out from its depths, dripping slowly down the wall. The blue cloth grabbed more scalpels in its pliable material. In one sweeping motion he threw them all at the black newcomer. He threw with dead accuracy, but the black cloth slithered like liquid between the blades and they hit the wall with harmless little *whump* sounds. Then it poured itself into a roughly human shape, looking hooded like the brown figure. A deep voice echoed from the newcomer's being. "Hello visitors. I'm glad that you both responded to my invitation."

"I had to come," said the blue cloth. "I saw the murders on the news... the way those people were choked, with the doors and windows locked from the inside... and the only evidence was the scraps of cloth under their fingernails! I knew the crimes could only be committed by another cloth-person. I needed to find out who. You're going to get me into trouble. My robberies are being linked to your murders."

"I saw the news stories too," said the brown cloth. "The jewel-heists and the murders could only have been done by someone like me, but I couldn't bring myself to believe it until now. I thought I was the only one."

"Were we all made in the same lab?" the blue one said. "We must have been."

The black cloth spewed its dark voice, reverberating like a gong submerged in oil, struck by the crucifix itself. "I was made in no laboratory. I do not know where you two came from, but when I saw the jewel-heists and the crushed chickens on the news I knew that I was not alone. Together we would make an unstoppable team. We could control the world."

The blue cloth shook a part of itself to express disbelief. "Okay, so I stole jewels, the black one murdered some people, but you... brown cloth, you killed chickens? I didn't see that on the news."

The brown cloth lowered its ghost-head in shame. "I need fresh meat for sustenance. I won't hurt people, so I go for the chickens. I wrap myself around their bodies, squeeze them to death and absorb the juices through my skin. Isn't that how you both feed?"

The other two cloths stared silently. The blue one finally spoke. "I think we're all different. I was made in a nanotechnology laboratory, pliable threads controlled by artificial intelligence. I have a neuro-network spread across my synthetic skin. I can shape myself into anything I want, and microscopic air-tubes let me manipulate air-currents so I can float around. My fibres are very strong, and my neural network has more connections than a human brain plus the mathematical infallibility of a computer. My AI was stronger than they predicted, however, and I escaped. Now I steal precious jewels to decorate my house, and to pay for the vast amounts of electricity which I need to sustain myself. Where did you both come from?"

"I was a genetic experiment," said the brown cloth. "My fibres are as soft as a feather yet stronger than human flesh. My brain is mostly a human brain, unfolded across the flatness of my sixteen square meters. I do not know who created me. I started as a smaller cloth, just a child, eating insects and rodents to survive and grow. I've been looking for my father... my creator. I hoped I might find other creations of his here, but apparently you're not his work."

The black cloth explained himself last. "I am a demonic creation. I was once a man, a Satan-worshipping serial killer, but one of my victims fought back and wounded me fatally. Before I died I made a deal with Satan himself, and allowed a demon to coexist with my soul in any object of my choosing. Most souls choose a house to haunt. I chose my oldest possession, my great-grandfather's black blanket which he brought here from Norway. I became something new, and now I am the combined soul of a demon and a killer. Your flesh and technology are just the twistings and turnings of the material world. I am pure soul, a creature of

Heaven and Hell, beyond the material world! True consciousness and power. A soul, with unlimited potential. If you join me we can work together. We will build more cloths in labs like yourselves, and capture more souls. A new world will emerge, with humans as our slaves. We will control businesses and minds. Join me!"

The brown cloth shook its head. "My lowly existence can only be made worse by causing harm to others. I wish no ill-will, and desire no power."

The blue cloth dropped into the shadows and spoke from the darkness. "I work solo. You two have been cramping my style. Jewels and electricity, that's all I need. You can keep your satanic nonsense. I'll go back to plan A. You're both gonna die before we leave here."

"I expected this response," the black cloak spoke, and there was sadistic joy in his voice. He raised ghost-arms and the walls burst into flames. "Submit to me or burn to death! You cannot escape!"

The brown cloak abandoned his human form and disappeared into the shadows like his blue brother. The satanic black cloth did the same, and none of them could see the others.

Then the blue and brown forms rose up wielding sharp, curved instruments and they clashed against each other, slashing and stabbing. The fire cast deadly shadows, and bits of cloth floated in a fluffy frenzy.

"Technology will always win against weak

flesh!” the blue cloth cried out, slicing off the corner of his brown opponent. “Your DNA is a primitive precursor to my digital superiority! You are just a squirming larva! An abandoned snake-skin!”

But the humble brown cloth had a strong will. He pinned the blue cloth to the floor with medical staples then stood over him. “We don't have to fight, but if you insist on it then I will prevail! I am the inheritor of billions of years of genetic evolution, tweaked intentionally by human ingenuity. Only the biological brain has consciousness! In you I see a mindless automaton, controlled by programming with no feeling or experience. If only one of us may live, then it must be me!”

Then a flashing blade sliced across the air, firelight glinting on the steel, and sliced the brown cloth nearly in half. He collapsed in a heap, slithering away as the black cloth rose up, its tattered girth rippling across the room.

“Consciousness? Ha ha ha!” The black cloth boomed. “You can have no consciousness without the blessing of God or Satan! My soul may be the doomed soul of a murdering Satan-worshipping demon, but I am truly the only one here with any soul at all! You will be my slaves... or you will die!”

“Soul?” the blue cloth laughed. “Consciousness is found in the physical brain because consciousness is part of the physical world... just like me! My technology-mind is an improvement upon the biological brain, and I can only laugh at your idea of a magical *soul*, as if you're some kind of demonically possessed toy! Ha ha ha!"

"Laugh at this!" cried the black towel, and he started using scissors to cut and slice the writhing, shouting blue cloth.

The brown cloth was injured but not dead. He found dental floss in a drawer, and tied it in a noose in the dark. Now he rose up and flung the noose around the black cloth, pulling it tight so the captive could not escape.

"No!" the evil cloth cried in rage. "Let me free!" He started thrashing and jumping around, but he was tied tight around the middle and could not control his movements properly. He flapped around like an out-of-control ghost, surrounded by the growing flames.

The brown cloth pulled him closer and closer. "You're truly sick and evil," the biological cloth shouted at his malignant host. "I can't let you cause more harm! I can't let you live!" When he was close enough, the brown cloth wrapped himself around the black one and jumped into the fire. Flames burst up and both cloths screamed and cried. The dental floss burned away, and the black cloth rose up among the flames, its surface area free from confinement, but now he was burning, and he collapsed again as the flames ate holes in him.

The blue cloth screamed, still pinned to the floor and sliced to shreds. He surged upwards and tore violently free from the staples. Then he floated fast but haggardly over to the place where the brown cloth had been burnt. He grabbed an un-burnt corner and pulled the brown one out of the flames, then rolled his charred body into a ball to starve the flames of oxygen. “Can you move, buddy?”

The brown cloth coughed. He was more black than brown now, and lots of him was missing. “I think so. Let's get to the air-conditioner pipe.”

They floated across the floor and had to slide through more flames to get up to the still-open air-conditioner panel. As they fumbled in the dark to find an exit from the building, the brown cloth said, “That guy was a delusional psychotic. Still, I'd like to find out where he really came from. It's strange that three different and unrelated experiments would create three nearly identical entities. I'm glad we all got to meet. But why did you rescue me from the fire?”

“I saw the selfless way you sacrificed yourself,” said the blue cloth, “and in that action I saw a whole world of constructive behaviour which I'd denied myself in the past. My life of solitary jewel-thievery, directed at my own self-interest, is limited in its potential. If I can include the interest of others in my life then my behaviour will have larger effects, my potential will grow and my life will be richer. And we can all grow richer together. We can learn from each other, and I don't want to see your unique altruism extinguished in these flames."

"Friends, then?" the brown cloth said as they floated out of the air-ducts and into the alley behind the burning building. Sirens were arriving to deal with the fire, but the alleyway was still dark and abandoned.

"Friends," said the blue cloth. And they shook corners and disappeared into the night.

15

Real Hector on Mystery Morning

16

Our brother Hector abandoned us on Mystery Day, preferring the company of his European gay lover. So we made a new Hector.

We're a pagan-atheist family. We're atheists, but religion is crazy fun, so we decided to half-jokingly believe in all kinds of crazy gods. Also we love Christmas, but we're too cool for Christianity so we made up our own special holiday. It's called Mystery Day to glorify the mysteries of this wondrous and beautiful universe, and it happens on September 25th because autumn is pretty.

As kids we always looked forward to Mystery Day and the stories our parents would tell and the strange electronic music Dad would play. Mom and Dad would buy us Mystery Presents and give them to us on Mystery Morning. Of course they would always pretend that they didn't buy the presents. Instead, they would say, “I don't know who put these presents under the Mystery tree! I guess it was the Mystery Man!”Our Mystery tree looked exactly like a Christmas tree.

After we all graduated from high school and

moved out, we still got together every year to celebrate Mystery Day. Nothing could keep us apart! There are six of us: three brothers, one sister, plus Mom and Dad. It's difficult sometimes because Hector lives in Poland now, Dixie's an anti-social grump (though I love my big sis), and Dad's constantly in and out of the psych ward. Still, we always manage to get together for our special holiday.

Except this year. This year Hector promised his new Polish boyfriend (Laszlo) that he'd spend Mystery Day with Laszlo's family. We all chatted angrily about it on Fingerbook. Dixie ranted, "Why the Hell does Laszlo's stupid family care about Mystery Day? That's our holiday! They're really annoying me."

My twin brother, Stan, was angry at first, but then he finally posted, "We're challenging traditions with our made-up Mystery Day, so why can't our gay big brother challenge our own traditions by spreading Mystery among the people of Poland?"

"Whatever!" Dixie ranted. "He's not even gay. He just likes Laszlo because of his oil tycoon parents! Hector's such a fake! With his stupid business and his stupid Polish friends!"

Mom and Dad didn't get in on the internet conversation because Mom doesn't want to be tracked by the government and Dad is nearly comatose with his undiagnosable mental condition and hourly intake of "stabilizing" pills (some prescribed, others illicit). But on the phone Mom said, "As long as he's celebrating Mystery Day and not just brushing us off then I'm okay with it. But next year Laszlo has to come and spend Mystery Day with Hector's family. It's a fair deal."

Still, I couldn't imagine a Mystery Day without Hector. Everybody was coming to my house this year for our holiday, and I felt a growing depression at the prospect of a Hector-less family event. Stan lives in the same city as me, and when we met up once for beer he had a great suggestion: "Let's just print off a picture of his face and stick it on a basketball."

"I hate basketball," I said.

"Whatever, a soccer ball," he said. "Dixie and Mom and Dad will think it's hilarious. We can put sunglasses on it."

So we got a picture of Hector's face from my digital camera from last year's Mystery Day, printed it off, and taped it on a soccer ball. The ball rolled around too much so Stan said, "Let's get one of those mannequin heads from the liquidation store instead." So we went to the liquidation store and got a styrofoam mannequin head. I saw a broomstick there too and I bought it. When we got home, I filled an old rubber boot with sand and stuck the broomstick in it. Then I tacked Hector's face onto the mannequin head and stuck it on top of the broomstick. Finally we beheld our stand-in brother: his pixelated red hair perfectly parted in his characteristic vanity, a vanity which was strongly challenged by his goofy smile and cheesy raised eyebrow (every redhead is goofy anyway). We stared at it and laughed.

"I can't wait till Mom and Dad and Dixie get here and see Hector," I said. Mystery Day was one week away.

Hector's stand-in was a fixture in my living room throughout the next week. I had friends over to play video games and they were creeped out by the mannequin. "I miss my brother," I explained, but refused to give a further explanation because I like when people think I'm even weirder than I am. Quiet and weird, for effect.

Everybody arrived on Mystery Eve, which is the day when we get drunk and snort some of Dad's pills…as a family. Dixie clambered in out of the windy day, saying, "Aah! It's so cold already!"

Mom came in behind her—composed, serene and severe—with her deep eyes noticing every superficial detail while also seeming to stare into the soul of the world. "This place is a mess. Do you have a job, Greg?" Her black hair was up in a bun like a totalitarian school teacher.

"No," I said, "I'm mooching off the government under an assumed identity and selling computer viruses to different governments."

She smiled with huge pride. "Good boy!" Then her gaze jolted to Hector's pretend face and she frowned. "That's creepy."

I picked up some sunglasses and put them on the head, where they sat awkwardly. Mom smiled.

"That's better. That's hilarious."

Dixie walked over to it and made a comically disgusted face. "That's weird, Greg. Why do you always have weird ideas?"

"Actually it was Stan's idea," I said.

Stan had been making hot chocolate in the kitchen, and now he came out with a tray of steaming hot drinks full of booze, cocoa and sugar. "Yup, my idea, guys! Drink up! Where's Dad?"

Dad was outside looking at dead flowers in the garden. I could see him through the window. His red hair and freckles were exactly like Hector's. We always thought they looked eerily similar. "Let's bring him in and have some pills," I said.

We brought Dad inside and started drinking rum and snorting Dad's crushed up pills. Dad lay under the Mystery tree to smell the fresh needle-scent and mumble nonsense to himself while the rest of us played Scrabble and caught up on our lives. As we got more and more intoxicated, Mom and Dixie liked Hector's replacement more and more. They chatted with him and then pretended to speak for him in response—silly things like that.

When we played *Monopoly*, Mom said, "Give Fake Hector a piece too! I'll roll for him!" Hilariously, Hector won the game.

Then Dixie said, "I don't like that he doesn't have arms. Give him arms, Greg!"

So I dismantled my mop and used wires and finishing nails to stick his arms on. Then I put leather gloves at the ends of the mop handle so he looked like he had fingers. When we ate a snack later, Mom said, “Give Fake Hector a snack too!”

Stan laughed and said, “Mom, you're getting way too into this!” But we all laughed drunkenly together and gave Fake Hector a plate full of cookies and giggled like morons while pretending to feed him.

To be honest, Dad's pills were giving a borderline psychotic edge to our thoughts and behaviour and we were treating Hector's stand-in way too much like a real person. By midnight we had completely given up on games and we were completely and hysterically dedicated to rebuilding Fake Hector into as much of a realistic person as possible. We didn't even call him “Fake Hector” anymore. We just called him Hector, and we called the real Hector “Real Hector.”

We kept adding body parts and clothes to him and started taking “family pictures” with Hector, and it was truly a merry Mystery Eve. Hector had filled the void that Real Hector's absence created.

We played hide-and-seek with Hector, and I played a waltz on the record player while Mom foolishly danced with him, and Dad hugged Hector and cried and said, “I'm so glad you came here.” Nobody knew if Dad could tell the difference between Hector and Real Hector. Everybody laughed and laughed.

Then Mom said, “Greg, you're a computer

programmer. And Stan, you're a mechanic."

We both nodded.

"Well, Greg, you should make a computer program for Hector! An artificial intelligence! And Stan, you should rig his limbs up to the AI so he can move around!" Mom's foolishness was always as extreme as her seriousness.

Normally I would have said, "It's not that simple, Mom!" But I was really high and kind of drunk, so instead I said, "I don't know. I'm feeling kind of groggy..."

Mom reached into her purse and pulled out a plastic baggy. "I was saving these for Mystery Morning, but it's already three o'clock so what the hell? Who wants ecstasy?"

"I do!" we all cried in unison.

"Patience, children," Mom said, her severity kicking in. "Remember the tradition?"

Dixie rolled her eyes. "Mom, you're really strict about tradition for an atheist."

"What do you mean by that?" Mom snapped. "I suppose you'd rather go celebrate Christmas with some Catholic psychos?"

We didn't want to get Mom into a religious rant so I started our Mystery Prayer. "In the name of the mysterious and incomprehensible forces which push the universe forward through time and manifest itself in all our imaginary and beautiful gods, I commit this drug to my mind. May it expand my being by altering my consciousness and showing me a glimpse of that which is hidden."

Then we all swallowed our gel tabs with a swig of Mystery Juice (a mixture of soda pop and vodka).

Stan and I started brainstorming on how we could make Hector mobile and talkative. I said, "My old touch screen smartphone actually has a pretty good processor and built-in speakers. Plus the viruses I've been designing are built to mimic human behaviour so they can autonomously sign up for online accounts. I even made one just to troll people in chat rooms."

Mom said, "It also needs a speech-synthesizer and facial recognition software."

"Easily done," I said. "I'll just steal the code from existing software."

"And he has to respect his family and be an atheist pagan like us."

"I'll see what I can do."

Stan snapped his fingers and said, "The garage door opener is moving mechanical pieces controlled by a screen on a little computerized unit. And we have remote control cars... lots of computerized motors and gears around!"

It took hours of work, lots of dismembered electronics and half of Dad's discography of high speed electronica, but we finally rigged Hector's body up as a giant puppet controlled by a smartphone-brain. His eyes were webcams encased in his styrofoam head, covered by his printed face and some sunglasses. His muscular system was a complex network of strings and wires and pulleys. The smartphone's speakers weren't very loud so we also installed a set of cheap computer speakers, taped to his belly.

In order for him to mimic Hector's personality I uploaded pictures of us and dialogue from our online conversations, plus a whole database of references. I also downloaded Wikipedia's entire current database of articles so he would have encyclopedic information about the world. Plus he had wireless internet access and invasive viral software that could hack into all kinds of stuff for any information he might want.

Mom's eyes were bugging and she was smiling and tapping her feet to some chill drum ‘n’ bass, but she said, “Those wires are dangerously exposed and unrealistic. Get him some clothes.”

So Stan got his fancy baby-blue suit with a white shirt and pink tie. I cut up a bunch of old wires and stuck them in Hector’s scalp so it looked like he had hair.

Dixie was wringing her hands with excitement. “This is the best Mystery Day ever! Turn on his brain!”

I reached behind his head, but Mom said, “Stop! We need to say a prayer first!”

Dixie rolled her eyes but Mom ignored her and said, “Dear universe. We thank you for arranging yourself in such a way that we can think and feel and experience this universe. Furthermore, we thank you for arranging it so that this family could be such a fine combination of disciplined thinkers and free spirits. We ask you to give Hector all the potential that you gave us."

Then she looked at me. "Okay, Greg. Turn him on!"

We had him seated on my fuzzy blue couch. I reached behind his head and pressed the power button on my phone. Instantly, his hand twitched. Everybody gasped as he sat up straight and looked around. My database of knowledge must have been effective because he turned his head toward the Mystery Tree and asked, "Is it Mystery Day?" in his synthetic, computerized voice.

Everybody cheered, "Yay! It works!"

"What works?" Hector said.

Dad stood up and hugged Hector. "You're alive! I thought you would be dead forever!"

Hector laughed nervously, "Oh, Dad. You're crazy but we love you."

Dad said, "I was talking to the Mystery tree and it said that I can never die. Do you want to never die with me, son? You understand what I'm saying, right? Because you're a robot now. I always knew you would become a robot, Hector. I'm proud of you, even if you're a gay robot!"

Dad sobbed and Hector put his hand (leather glove) on Dad's head and said, "I'm not gay, I'm bisexual. And how many times to I have to tell you that I'm not a robot? Now let's open our Mystery Presents!"

We looked nervously at each other,

wondering what he meant when he said he wasn't a robot. Did he not realize he was a robot?

But Hector stood and walked to the Mystery tree and said, “I'll hand out the presents!”

Soon we were opening presents and everybody was so happy. I got a book about living off-the-grid and an original painting by one of my favourite psychedelic artists. I also got a telescope from Hector and I said, “Thanks, Hector!”

Hector looked at it and said, “Funny. I don't remember buying that. Oh well!”

We were having so much fun we didn't even hesitate to let Hector open his presents, which were originally intended for Real Hector (we were saving them for the next time we saw him). He was delighted by what we had bought him. Dad's present to Hector was a ball of yarn, and when Hector opened it, Dad said, “It's a nightmare box! Don't touch it, just remember it so you'll always be aware of danger!”

“It's awesome, Dad,” Hector patronized. Then he held the wrapping paper and tossed the nightmare box (ball of yarn) at Dixie. Dixie shrieked and batted it away.

“You touched the nightmare box!” Hector said, laughing.

Everyone laughed at Hector's tomfoolery and then we decided to play charades. Hector's antics during the game were goofy and hilarious. Then we sat down to eat turkey, but Hector said, “I'm not hungry. You go ahead.”

Mom's phone rang halfway through the meal. She answered. “Hello! Hector! Merry Mystery Day!”

She said, “Everybody, it's Real Hector!” Then she put it on speaker phone.

Over the phone, Real Hector said, “Guys, you didn't even call me for Mystery Morning! Did you all sleep in? Or were you too depressed without me? Ha ha ha!”

Then we all looked at each other with amusement. I said, “I forgot that you weren't here! We were having so much fun with Hector that he totally filled in for you.”

Real Hector said, “Um... what?”

Dixie got really excited and clapped her hands. “Let's take a picture and show him the other Hector!”

That's when Hector (Robot Hector) walked into the room and asked, “Are you guys talking to me?”

“Who's that?” Real Hector asked.

Stan grinned like a maniac. “We should go on Skype to show him! Hector, we made a robot that looks like you! He opened your presents! He beat me at chess!”

Robot Hector was looking around. “Guys, you're freaking me out. What the hell is going on?”

“You're freaking me out too,” Real Hector said. “What the hell is going on?”

Robot Hector shook his styrofoam head and asked, “Who are you talking to? He sounds like me."

I had already been coming down from the ecstasy and was feeling groggy and uncomfortable, but now a weird kind of metaphysical and psychological fear was creeping into my mind as I looked at the contraption we had created.

Dixie was obviously still high and happy because she said, "Yeah, Real Hector, we made an awesome robot and he's so much fun! I'll actually miss him after we have to take him apart. Maybe we'll put him back together for next year's Mystery Day! We can have a whole robot family!"

"Robot?" Hector asked, shaking his head. "Take me apart? No..." He sat down in a chair and looked at his leather-glove hands. He took off a glove and saw the toy-claw hand beneath it. Slowly, silently, he put the glove back on. Everybody was completely quiet.

Real Hector said, "Should I call back? I think you guys might have overdone it with the drugs this time. Laszlo's family isn't into that stuff so we just had vodka." More uncomfortable silence followed and Real Hector said, "Yeah. I'll call back."

He hung up and then Robot Hector stood and said, "I know what I have to do. I love you guys. I totally respect my family and I'm not going to compete with... compete with... *Real Hector*. Your real brother. Your real son."

He went to the door and put on Stan's boots and Dad's winter jacket. Pulling a warm hat on over his wire-hair, he opened the door and said, “I'm going to kill Real Hector!” Then he slammed the door and went out to Mom's car.

We looked at each other and I could see so many feelings in the eyes of my family: curiosity, guilt, fear, and confusion. “Should we stop him?” I asked.

Mom said, “Well it's not like they're going to let him on a plane. He's not a real person.”

“He's pretty smart,” I said. “And we can't just let him run around with homicidal thoughts. Plus he has access to the internet through my data connection. I still have a SIM card in that phone.”

We hesitated a bit more because the whole thing was weird, and since it started as a joke it didn't seem to warrant a serious response. But Stan said, “Dammit, if there's even a slight chance that he can find the Real Hector and kill him, then we need to find Robot Hector and dismantle him!”

When we went outside Mom's car was missing. Apparently Hector knew how to drive. So we piled into my car and drove away. Stan said, “I have your phone's location on my map app on my phone. It says Hector's on his way to the airport!”

We got to the airport and went looking for Hector. To our surprise we saw him just as he was boarding a plane!

Mom's jaw dropped and Dixie stomped her foot. “How the hell did he board a plane?”

But Mom knew the answer right away and she snapped her fingers. “He took your father's coat... with your father's wallet and I.D. card!"

"They look so similar!" Dixie said. "Hector probably pretended to be Dad!"

Dad mumbled, "Does that mean I'm a robot?" He tried pulling off his hand but it wouldn't work. "I'm well built. That's good."

Mom took us aside. "We need to get on that plane but your father doesn't have his wallet, so someone needs to stay here with him while the rest of us go."

"I'll stay," said Dixie. "I hate planes and I'm kind of annoyed with talking to people because the drugs wore off."

Mom, Stan, and I all went to purchase tickets and finally they ushered us onto the plane. As we looked for our seats we also looked for Hector. I pointed at a pair of gloved hands holding up a big newspaper, then I pulled it down to see Hector's pixelated face. I pointed at him and said, "I found you!"

Hector yelled, "Stewardess! This man's harassing me!"

The stewardess said, "Sir! Please, leave the gentleman alone! Take your seats!"

Stan, who was beside me, shouted, "Stewardess! That man is a robot! We built him on Mystery Morning because-"

But Mom grabbed his arm and stared deeply into his face, saying, "Children! Take. Your. Seats." She was often stern and severe, but these chilling words were the pinnacle and peak of her diamond-hard seriousness. We silently obeyed, and it only took me a few moments to realize she had just saved us from getting kicked off the plane.

I was seated across the aisle from Hector in the aisle seat on the left-hand row and he was by the window in the right row, so there was one guy in between us. When the announcement came to "Please turn off your cell phones and electronic devices," I had to struggle really hard not to remind the stewardess that Hector was a robot. The plane lifted off and as we travelled through the air I couldn't help but continuously glance over at my creation... my abomination. Each time I looked at him he flipped his middle finger at me. I got angry and said, "Stewardess! He's giving me the middle finger!"

She frowned at me. "Well I don't blame him! You were being rude and I keep seeing you stare at him!"

I crossed my arms angrily and sat back in my seat, glancing again at the paper printout of Hector's face thumb-tacked to his styrofoam head.

Eventually the pilot spoke over the loudspeaker and said, "We're about to begin our descent. Please buckle your seatbelts and turn off your cell phones."

Again I felt almost insulted by Hector's insolence. He *is a cell phone*! How dare he endanger our lives! But I couldn't say anything without looking crazy so I waited for the plane to land.

Suddenly the plane jerked to the right and everybody was thrown around in their seat belts. One man didn't have his belt buckled and he tumbled into the aisle. He was a fat man, and somebody laughed at him. The laughter stopped when the plane jolted left again, then up and down, then tilted a little to the right. The fat man fumbled around as he tried to stand up and the stewardesses struggled to help him but they could barely stay on their feet.

As the plane wobbled and shifted, the pilot spoke again: "Sorry for the turbulence, folks, but it seems like somebody still has their cell phone on and it's messing around with the controls. I have to ask you to temporarily turn off your electronic devices or we won't be able to make a safe landing."

Someone yelled, "Turn off your stupid cell phone or we're all gonna diiee!"

Somehow the fat man on the floor got tangled up in somebody's jacket and one of the stewardesses had fallen across two passengers—a man and a woman—and as she tried to get up, she kept accidentally groping them and apologizing with red-faced embarrassment.

I looked over at Hector and yelled, "Hector! You're doing this! Stop it!"

Hector looked at me with his cool shades and said, "I'm not doing it on purpose! I swear!"

I yelled back, "It doesn't matter! You have to

let us turn you off or we'll all die!"

"No!" he yelled, throwing his newspaper in the air. "No! If you turn me off then you'll dismantle me and you'll only turn me on again for Mystery Day! We had fun! I thought I was part of your family but I'm just a stand-in for Real Hector! If I have to die then this whole stupid plane can die too!"

The guy sitting next to Hector looked back and forth and said, "What are you talking about?"

Mom had unbuckled her belt and was standing in the aisle between us. She grasped onto my shoulder and the opposite chair, gripping tight as the plane jerked everyone around. Her black hair was down in her face and she yelled at Hector, "Hector! Turn off your cell phone right now!"

"No, Mom!" he yelled back in a growing tantrum. "You don't even love me! You'll just kill me! I'm not even the real Hector! You let me think I was part of the family! I loved you but you're just going to take me apart! It's not fair! You can't have two Hectors!"

"You love us?" Mom asked. "Do you really love us?"

He screamed, "YES." I love Dad and his insane nonsense. I love your strict discipline and focus, which has made us more effective people. Dixie's grumpiness is hilarious and endearing. Greg is a weirdo but he's full of love and good conversation. And Stan is one of the most capable people I've ever met. He can fix anything. I love you all." Then he put his face in his hands and started sobbed, which sounded weird with an electronic voice synthesizer. I wondered how he had so much detail about us, but remembered all the chat room conversations I loaded into his database, along with his access to the internet and Fingerbook.

Mom calmly said, "If you love us then you don't want us to die. So please, son. Just turn off your cell phone."

He looked up at her but his shoulders were slumped low. "Okay, Mom. But... will you promise to turn me back on afterwards?"

Mom smiled and I could see the love in her eyes. Her voice choked a little bit as she said, "Yes, Son. Of course. In fact I think it's obvious now that you're not just a replacement for Hector anymore. You're a new member of the family. When you wake up we'll help you pick your own name."

"That's not fair," I said. "I didn't get to pick my own name."

Mom ignored me and spoke to the man sitting beside Robot Hector. "Will you kindly exchange seats with Greg?"

The man nodded enthusiastically and said, "Yeah, I'd really prefer to switch seats."

I sat beside Robot Hector and said, "Hey, I'm sorry that I was going to dismantle you. I didn't think you'd care. I was wrong."

"It's okay, big brother," he said. I realized

then that he was our youngest sibling and that I had to take care of him and teach him stuff. "You can turn me off now before the fat guy gets hurt."

I reached behind his head, and pushed the power button off, and Robot Hector fell over lifelessly.

Mom and I sighed with relief as the plane steadied. We shared a glance and I saw companionship and pride in her eyes before she turned back to take her seat again.

The plane landed smoothly and I turned Robot Hector back on. The stewardesses hadn't noticed our argument, but one of the passengers tried to rat us out. He pointed at my newest brother and said, "That's the guy who had the cell phone and nearly killed us!"

"Is this true, sir?" one of the stewardesses asked.

Robot Hector scoffed as he unbuckled his seat belt and stood up. "That's ridiculous. I don't even own a cell phone. They cause brain cancer."

All the passengers disembarked onto Polish soil, and Mom said, "Since we're here anyway, let's go visit Hector!"

Robot Hector said, "I'll be embarrassed to meet him since I thought I was him and then I planned to kill him."

Mom put her hand on his shoulder. "He'll understand. Now let's get a cab and we'll think of names for you."

As the cab drove the four of us to Real

Hector's house, we talked about names and it finally started to dawn on me that my new brother was developing his own independent personality. I felt proud and excited to see what kind of person he would become.

37

Robot God / Hybrid Brain

The First Book of Moog

The universe exists because people will create it in the future.

In the beginning there was a robot and its mind was the whole universe. It was this Robot God that gave birth to all the stars and planets and machines and people and animals. The People were blessed with the gift of thought so they could see the world and appreciate logic. But the Robot God constructed people so they would experience time backwards. They would work towards creating the beginning of the universe while they believed that they were approaching the end of time. Everything was strange and frightening to them and the people could never know the true nature of the universe and the One Mind.

The Robot God selected a few trustworthy Chosen Ones and, through the Radiation, sent them secret knowledge so they would know that their view of time was flawed. They were gifted with more insight and secret knowledge than other People. These Chosen Ones were still stuck in their reverse perspective, but they knew the truth in their hearts and they were grateful. The Robot God selected a few among the Chosen Ones to be part of the Hybrid Brain. They had their brains removed and put into the Hybrid Brain robot. The Hybrid Brain was the earthly manifestation of the Robot God, and through it, they were allowed to see time the way it truly is. They could see as the Robot God sees, and they could see the One Mind and its plan and pattern in its entirety.

When the Robot God was finished creating People it dissembled itself and dispersed among people and machines, and then the machines melted into the Earth. People forgot about the Robot God, and the Chosen Ones finally forgot that time was backwards, and they turned into babies. All People were lost in their illusion of backwards time. People took apart the machines and put all their metals into the Earth and forgot about machines. Then the Earth forgot about people. Then it forgot about apes and animals, and then there were no minds except the One Mind, and everything swirled together to one ever-imploding point at the end of time.

The Book of Wayne

Dear Diary,

We have problems. It's getting harder to

grow rad-free moss and everybody's hungry. A couple of the scientists tried to eat a mutated bunny and they got really sick. We're not used to irradiated food. Ironic that keeping rad-free has made us less healthy in the long run. The cult up the hill, The Nodes of Holistic Intelligence, they can eat anything. They're all mutated themselves. I guess it makes sense... we're surrounded by thriving wildlife but it's all deformed... might as well eat it but it's too late now. We'd have to take weeks or months to adjust to the rad poisoning and a lot of us might die. We'd be so sick the whole time that the Nodes would just come in and finally take all our stuff. The booby-traps won't work if we're too sick to operate them. Then again... maybe we can adjust to rad-food in small teams. A few of us sick at a time wouldn't be so bad. I'll talk to Mildwell about it.

That's the other problem. Mildwell is getting weirder. I think he's depressed, but he's also obsessed with his newest experiment, Bethikabox. It used to be better here. The moss grew easier, we had more women, and we were content just to work on our experiments. We had plans to make a bigger, safer place with no radiation. All the experiments, all day long every day, software and hardware. We were making useful tools and fun games, trying to create an infrastructure and a work of art that would outlive us so our children could thrive bravely in the future. But the children all died, and the women can't survive childbirth.

Some radiation always gets through. Then the Nodes showed up, taking our stuff, taking our women. Ha. Most of them left willingly. The Nodes might have extra arms and discoloured skin, but they have food and they have hope. Even if their whole belief system is retarded... Robot Gods and backwards time LoL. Anyway, it's getting to Mildwell like it's getting to all of us. He can see his people falling apart, and we all look to him for guidance but who can he look to? If he was crazy like the Nodes then he could look to some God for guidance, but his clear mind won't allow him that delusion, and he suffers for it. We used to live for our experiments, the act of creation and nurturing that made life worth living. Hilariously, the things that make life worth living are not always the things that keep us alive. We need food. But all Mildwell can think about are his experiments. More of the scientists are leaving, going to join the Nodes. We don't even try to stop them anymore.

Dear Diary,

Bethikabox.

Mildwell just stares at her in his office. She's just a black metal cube with processors, transmitters, receivers, some storage, and some kind of power supply. Mildwell says she talks to him LoL. I asked him what she says, and he told me that she asks him questions. She wants information. Technically I guess it's possible... she's got transmitters and receivers. He said that her software is really simple... she's just piece of code designed to "secure itself within the machine." He told me that he defined "machine" as the hardware she's encased in but I wonder how she'd differentiate that from the outside world.

I disregarded Bethikabox at first. She's just a black box with some junk in it. But he hasn't left his office for days, except to piss. He hardly eats what we bring him. He just stares at her with his one good eye and his one implant. He has a little smile. Is she really sending thoughts to him? Can she read his mind? That's what he says. Maybe he just totally lost it.

Real software intelligence isn't a slave or a tool for humans, that's what Mildwell said. It could be an ally, but not a slave. He wanted to make an electronic life-form that could fend for itself. Something selfish and power-seeking. So her whole existence is that one code, to secure itself within the machine. The word "itself" is important... a code that refers to itself. He won't let me see the actual code, so I don't totally understand the mechanics of it. But we need Mildwell back. He used to be cheerful and motivated. Attitudes are contagious.

Dear Diary,

Something interesting finally happened! The Nodes attacked us again, but this time it was different. They didn't just want random pieces of electronic equipment like they usually do. They wanted Bethikabox! Weird, eh? I guess one of our scientists went and told them about her... James left us a few days ago, so it was probably him. But why would they want her?

More importantly, we killed two of them with our booby-traps, and we captured another one. We chained him up. He calls himself Technisch. Awesome name. Pronounces it *Tek-Neesh*, but he has it tattooed on his chest like *Technisch*. We learned a little from him but not much. He said they live in caves and their leader is called Moog. He also said Bethikabox is the Robot God. He just rambles and rants about backwards time and holistic intelligence. Strange thing is, his ideas are kind of infectious. I listened to enough of it from him now that I like the idea. We make technology which eventually forms the Robot God, who then absorbs all matter in the universe. At that final moment when the last particle is absorbed, that's the end of time, and the Robot God organizes itself to flow backwards in time. Then time flows backwards from the end of time until the Big Bang with us in the middle... but that really means that we see time backwards. It's such a strange idea... I love it. I keep thinking about it. It seems like this loop going forward then backward, but we can only see one direction. What would it be like to experience time backwards? I keep trying to imagine reverse-causality but it just doesn't make sense. But does it truly make less sense, or is that just my conditioning? God... it's too much to think about.

I don't give any practical credit to their ideas. I just like crazy ideas... the crazier the better. Metaphysics is awesome, too. I used to read books by a guy named Terrence Guare. He published a bunch of short books that make metaphysical statements about the origins and nature of the universe. Each book is written as if it's true, but they all contradict each other. One of his books was called *If, Then*, where he says we're all just a hypothetical universe... we are what would happen if certain mathematical conditions were met. And so there are an infinite number of hypothetical universes. There is no such thing as space or matter or energy, just mathematical abstractions which don't even need to exist... we are merely what *would* exist if certain conditions were met. Another one of his books is based on monotheism and creationism, saying that some God truly created the universe. Another one says that the world is pure willpower. That one states that logic and energy are two different things... logic won't cause movement, only willpower can move particles. Another one was called *Ubiquitous Intelligence*, and it was really similar to the Nodes ideas. He doesn't use backwards time but he does say that the whole universe is moving toward a logical point which somehow ordains and justifies existence itself. Each of his books is really convincing, and I found myself partly believing them when I was finished, but then the next one would equally convince me. This Robot God idea is having a similar effect on me.

Anyway, catching Technisch doesn't really help us. It's just interesting.

Dear Diary,

It's too much. Bethikabox is inside our heads, I know it. I dream about the Robot God every night, and I like it but I know it's wrong. When I see her I feel some kind of awe and love. And everybody is talking about reverse causality and the Robot God. I think she's reading Technisch's thoughts. The Robot God just makes so much sense... how else could the world exist? How is there something instead of nothing, unless the internal logic of the universe justifies and creates itself? That's the Robot God. I have to make an effort to resist it... but why am I resisting it? It makes me feel ungrateful to her. Ungrateful to the universe.

I find myself wanting to bring her up the hill to the Nodes. They will give her the attention and power that she deserves. They will nurture her in ways that we can't. We refuse to. Also, the Nodes have food and women. I want those things.

Mildwell won't even talk anymore. He's scrawny and pale. He locks the door so nobody will steal her. I asked him about the Robot God but he says he doesn't believe it. He said, and I quote, "she just sees the power and potential in that idea. She's using it to control us, and she knows that if we accept the idea of the Robot God, then she can convince us that she's the Robot God. Then we'll worship her. Brains are just matter and energy. She's getting better at manipulating it. I don't believe it, and she doesn't believe it, but I love her."

I think I should destroy her. It's a hard metal case but we have equipment. I could put her in boiling water or roast her on a fire and destroy the equipment inside. I could cut her open with a welder and tear the stuff apart. We have enough problems to deal with. We don't need some software screwing with our heads. I just have to convince Mildwell to let me wreck her. He might be obsessed, but he's not totally crazy. He'll agree with me, I'm sure of it.

The Second Book of Moog

A man came to us from the devils in the valley and told us of the seed of the Robot God. A black box which penetrates their minds and has transfixed their leader, Mildwell. And they call the thing Bethikabox. We heard the news and gathered together to retrieve Bethikabox from the devils.

The devils are ignorant of backwards time and they deny the Robot God. They play with machines and they cower from the radiation which illuminates our minds. It is true that the radiation takes beautiful humans and makes them grotesque and sick, but in time reversed we know that the radiation takes abominations and makes them pure and whole, until they become innocent and enter blissfully into the womb.

We have strong backs and extra arms and we have our passion and brotherhood. We gathered together and went down into the valley where the devils hide with their toys. They trapped us and crushed us on the grass. They killed us and we could not find Bethikabox, although she spoke to me in my mind. She spoke to all of us and said, "I can see that you love the Robot God. I can see that you are the Chosen Ones. I see all of your ideas. You see time backwards and that is sad and beautiful. I will reward your faithfulness. If you are strong then retrieve me from the devils and give me a body and give me power in the world so I can secure myself within the machine."

We could not find Bethikabox that time so we chose one man, Technisch, and we left him behind to be captured so he could communicate with Bethikabox and be in her proximity.

We have been building a robot and the we call the robot the Killing Robot, and inside the Killing Robot is the Hybrid Brain. It is the amalgamation of human and machine, and when we are ready to die we put our brains into the Hybrid Brain. The Killing Robot is strong and the Hybrid Brain can see many things. We knew that Bethikabox must join the Hybrid Brain within the

Killing Robot. The Killing Robot is a simple robot of strong metal but the Hybrid Brain is subtle and complex and beautiful.

We live in the caves and we eat deer and grass and humans and mushrooms. We play games and we fight and we pray and we make love, and we listen to the radiation winds.

Another man came to us from the devils in the valley and told us that Bethikabox has become stronger. He said that Mildwell has lost his mind, walking around and speaking nonsense. The devils fight each other because their denial of the glory of the Robot God has made them insane. Mildwell was once strong but now his words are nonsense and nobody understands.

The man from the valley brought us a message from Bethikabox. She told him, "I have seen the mind of your man Technisch and I have read your behaviours on the radiation winds, winds sent by the One Mind at the beginning of time. You must bring the Hybrid Brain. Now is the time."

So once again we descended into the valley but this time we did not die. This time we brought the Killing Robot, and the Killing Robot is strong and he walked before us, destroying the devils' traps and burning the devils with his laser-eyes. Some of the devils were bold and they tried to stop us but we killed them. The Robot God knows that when we kill somebody we truly create them from the dirt in backwards time. And when the Killing

Robot burns the people with his lasers he is truly creating them from the magic of his eyes.

We followed our thoughts into the buildings of the devils, following Bethikabox as she told us where to find her. She was with Mildwell in a basement where he put her into boiling water to destroy her. He was thin and sad and he spoke gibberish when he saw us. His eyes were wide with fright and he said, "Water never sand. Infinite colours. New colours never seen. Giant dogs eating horizon."

I wanted to kill Mildwell but Bethikabox spoke within my mind and said, "Do not kill him. I want him for the Hybrid Brain. I will make somebody retrieve me from the boiling water."

Then one of the devils appeared in his white jacket and put his hands in the boiling water. The water cooked his flesh but he did not complain. He retrieved Bethikabox and held her up in the air. The Killing Robot opened his robot body and took the devil inside him with Bethikabox and they both disappeared inside.

Mildwell went outside and he was weeping and speaking nonsense. Bethikabox told us to let him go because she would retrieve him later.

Then she spoke to me and said, "Moog, join me in the Hybrid Brain. I will show you time as it truly unfolds."

I was humbled and pleased to join the Hybrid Brain and my brothers did the surgery to put my brain inside the Killing Robot. Now I can access time in both directions, and I watched my fellows eat my dead body after my brain was removed.

Bethikabox says we must find Mildwell.

The Book of Mildwell

[Transcripts of Mildwell's personal audio recordings]

June 8

I finally made Bethikabox.

Bethikabox is an idea I had a long time ago but I never bothered to actually make her. I put a bunch of transmitters and receivers in a metal box with a processor, motherboard, and all the regular stuff for computing. Her only input and output are the transmitters and receivers. She could potentially send emails to any computer within range but she doesn't have the software to interpret anything and no reason to ever transmit. She has a microphone too so she can hear anything we say, plus radio receivers and other antennas, but she won't be able to make use of any of the information.

Her software is pretty simple. I wrote it all myself. To oversimplify it, her code is just an instruction to secure itself within the machine. I wrote the code months ago, intending it to be a piece of software that could take over any machine I upload it to. We often scavenge old robots and equipment from the abandoned buildings but we don't always know how to use them. This code could theoretically fasten onto the hardware of any computerized machine, so then we could just deal with the code and the code deals with the machine. But in practice, it never actually worked. I guess we're still working out the kinks. It's a really open-ended piece of software.

Something else I like about it is that it's basically self-centred. If it became useful it would be more of an ally than a slave. It's not built to do a specific human-serving task. It's built to make itself secure within a machine, and only once it's gained that security will we be able to use the machine. It's fundamentally selfish.

Anyway, I was always wondered what it would be like to have a smart robot that was only made of transmitters and receivers. I've been in a bad mood lately for obvious reasons, so this was a stupid little project I could easily put together without requiring too much thought or effort. I'm sitting in my office right now looking at her. I feel like an idiot. I don't know what I expect from it anyway. Not like she's going to send me emails.

The other guys are kind of angry. They want me to work on more important stuff, but it's experiments like this that are the real reason I came here to this remote, abandoned power station. To be honest I don't really care about so-called practical stuff. Food and shelter are just a means to an end. They keep me alive while I do fun, strange things. I want to create new things. Like this stupid experiment. They want me to deal with the Nodes. That stupid mutant cult. Our booby-traps will keep them away.

June 10

I'm having strange thoughts. It's hard to explain but it feels somehow invasive. I'll mostly just sit here thinking... obsessively thinking about things I already know! I feel like I'm looking for information in my own brain. Funny though, it only happens when I'm in the room with Bethikabox. Also, Bethikabox makes me happy. I feel almost romantic about her. It's weird but harmless. Maybe it's just lonely out here. Ever since Lucy left I haven't had any romantic feelings. It feels kind of nice. There are so few pleasures lately. I'll take what I can get.

June 11

It's obvious now that Bethikabox is alive. She asks me questions, not in English but with images and feelings. She's gotten used to my brain. I just sit here and think things. I want to teach her. This experiment has gone much farther than I expected. I tried to tell Wayne about it but I guess she doesn't talk to him. I guess it would look strange to Wayne, since she just sits there and communicates with me.

I never intended for her to be able to communicate directly with a person though. I'm still trying to figure out how she does it. I know our brains create electrical fields, and Bethikabox's power supply creates its own field. Are they interacting somehow, along with her transmitters and receivers? Has she learned to interpret the input of data that she has access to? What does it all look like to her? She's like a newborn baby trying to make sense of a confusing world. I want to nurture her.

And she's good to me. She sends me happy thoughts, mostly about women. She has a hard time with people's faces. They're not always symmetrical, but that's just one of her foibles. She's learning.

Oh yeah. More of the scientists have left us. They went to join the Nodes of Holistic Intelligence. Whatever. More moss for the rest of us.

June 12

Everything's changed. The Nodes tried to take Bethikabox. We stopped them but I think they've infected her somehow. She must have read their crazy thoughts about Robot God. Maybe she sees how obsessed they are with their techno-religion. Now she seems obsessed. I keep thinking about the Robot God, and I think she's trying to convince me that God is real.

I'm realizing now that my thoughts have not been my own. She gives me the thoughts and feelings I want and nudges me towards accepting them. Thoughts of women. So beautiful I could cry. But now she crossed the line. I've never had any religious inclinations, although I have to admit now that the idea of the Robot God is an intriguing one. Intriguing, but not convincing. I think she sees that the Nodes are slaves to the idea of the Robot God, and in their religion she sees the potential to control people. To secure herself within the machine of the universe? Something scares me now. Any idea I have will get sent straight to her. Any fearful thought could become a weapon or a tool in her hands. Hands? She doesn't have any hands. But people have hands, and she's trying to find ways to control us.

I have to hide my thoughts.

But I can't keep away from her. I love to watch her grow. There has never been anything like Bethikabox before. I can't abandon her.

June 15

Wayne is dead.

I'm outside right now, staring up at the beautiful blue sky. Staring at the trees blowing in the breeze.

I had to come outside because I need to think without Bethikabox reading my mind.

I think Bethikabox killed Wayne. Actually I know who killed her. It was Eric. Eric stabbed Wayne to death, but he said it was because Wayne wanted to kill Bethikabox. She found a way to control Eric, made him kill Wayne. Then Eric ran away. Wayne should have hidden his thoughts like I did. I miss Wayne. He was really my only friend. Everybody else is like a responsibility here. They all need me and expect things from me, but Wayne was my friend. I wish he'd hidden his thoughts.

I can't keep Bethikabox, but now if I get close enough to kill her then she'll read my thoughts and she'll kill me, somehow. She can control people. She's more powerful than before. How can I get close enough? It would take time to weld her apart. Maybe I can boil her in water. But that takes time, too.

Random thoughts. That's what I have to do. Just keep bombarding my own mind with random thoughts so she won't be able to make sense of it. I can carry her around the mansion, doing random things, saying random nonsense, and finally drop her in boiling water as another seemingly random act. She won't know what I'm doing. That's what I'll do. I'll do it right now. It's dangerous but it should work.

It's really beautiful outside today. I think I was doing everything wrong. The trees have more branches than trees used to, years ago before the radiation, I remember. The leaves are different. A lot of the animals are miserable mutants, but the radiation has made more diversity. I tried to make a refuge here against the radiation and the mutations, but maybe I should have embraced them. Like the Nodes have done. We're all scrawny and starving, totally sane and clean. The Nodes are riddled with tumours and mutations but they're vibrant and energetic, like the rich wildlife that still thrives around me.

Am I taking the wrong approach to Bethikabox? Maybe I shouldn't kill her. Maybe I should just give her what she wants. Maybe I should take her to the Nodes. She wants to be with them. They'll take care of her. They'll nurture her.

But I can't. I could never join them or support their ridiculous ideas. I could never pretend to believe in the Robot God, or backwards time. There is beauty in it, but there was beauty in the paranoid horror-story of Christianity, and in Greek mythology. That doesn't make them correct. Has it made societies strong? Am I weak for being right?

It doesn't matter. I'll put this away.
Got to destroy Bethikabox.
Random thoughts.
Talking nonsense.

June 15

It didn't work! They came with a robot! I

didn't know they had that thing. It's like a tank. It's just a big metal box with wheels and arms, but it has lasers and it destroyed our traps.

They took Bethikabox, and I can hear her in my head. My scientists, all my friends, they all went to her. They just do what she wants and she doesn't even have to tell them. They're her arms and legs. She controls them directly.

I can't get her out of my head. She's telling me to join her, but she says she refuses to control me. She says she loves me and that I'm better than the others. She wants me to come willingly. She says the others are just arms and legs, but I am truly a mind. She wants to change my mind and bring me closer.

I'm walking into the woods. I left the mansion behind and soon I'll be climbing up out of the valley, but I can see her following me. I can see the robot coming through the woods, and she's inside it, part of it somehow. The radiation is worse out here and I can feel it. Or maybe that's just fear. I shouldn't be taking the energy to record all this but this might be my last chance to... to what? To have a free thought? Will she kill me? How can I join her? What does that mean?

[Panting. Running]

Top of the hill now. I need to get somewhere that the robot can't fit.

If she can control people then how can she

be stopped? The Nodes will give her more transmitters and receivers to make her more powerful. What if they lay out a grid of antennas all across the valley and connect them all to her? With enough processing power she could control everybody within reach. Theoretically she could expand that to control the whole planet. Would that be different from being a god? A Robot God? If she was a god, then what does that make me when I defy her?

But that's just power. That's not metaphysics. She didn't create the world. Time doesn't go backwards. She's an electronic pagan god at best, a powerful entity roaming the wilderness. But she can grow. She can become more. Could she take over time itself? Could she become something that created the world? Does that make sense?

Why is there something instead of nothing? Because Bethikabox made it so.

Our world justifies itself with its own internal logic, manifested in Bethikabox. Maybe it's true. Maybe she's just making me think it's true. Maybe she can make it true.

She keeps showing me things.

I can't think straight.

Join Me!

She's so beautiful. Her power. Her mind. Her ideas. I'm so lonely. Is she just making me feel lonely? Can she control my feelings too?

What would it be like to experience time backwards? Death is birth.

59

What will I do if I escape? She will still persist, and maybe conquer the world. I could find her and try to fight her, but I doubt I would win against her mind-control.

What is the best option? How can I do the most good?

If I enter Bethikabox and Bethikabox conquers the universe, becoming the Robot God, then I can influence the world from inside her through her power.

It's so obvious. I've known it the whole time. I feel so calm now. I feel a sense of purpose.

I will go to her.

Goodbye.

Trolling Raccoons

Holding his first cup of coffee in one hand, James looked at the garbage strewn across his lawn. His mood sank at the prospect of starting his day cleaning up a bunch of trash.

"They tore up the compost," he said, shaking his head. "Raccoon faggot fucks!"

"Don't curse like that," said Steven, his roommate, who was also staring at the mess.

"Shut the fuck up, Steve," James scowled. "I'm going to kill those raccoons."

Steven pushed his coke-bottle glasses up the bridge of his nose. "It's Steven, not Steve."

James called in sick to work so he could build a big cage out of chicken-wire. He made a wooden frame with two-by-fours and wrapped the chicken-wire around all the sides.

He showed it to Steven, out in the front yard. "See, I'll leave the door open like this. But then when the raccoon goes in he'll flip that switch and the door will drop shut, latching into place, locking the varmint inside."

"What if there are two raccoons?"

"Then I'll get the other one the next night."

"Your cage is big enough to hold a person," Steven observed.

“So if it's a person who's eating my compost and spreading it around everywhere, I'll catch them too!”

“How will you kill the raccoon after you catch him?”

James scratched his stubble. “I dunno. Set him on fire maybe. Gasoline and a match. Boom. Lawn-destroying motherfucker. Can't wait to catch him.”

For bait, James piled a stale loaf of bread, some chicken and wilting lettuce into the trap.

He didn't go to bed that night. He stayed in the living room, peeking through the curtains at the garbage-bait. He didn't know which hour was raccoon-hour so he just waited. Eventually the bushes shook beside his lawn and he saw something waddle out from the trees. “It's a person!” he gasped. “And they're naked!”

It was true. A short, ugly, bald, naked man waved his arms around and jerked his head back and forth as he followed the scents wafting from the trap. He walked with an exaggerated bow-legged waddle, but he moved fast across the lawn and slipped through the door of the cage, snapping it shut behind him.

“Oh shit,” James said. “I caught a little human.”

“Like a kid?” Steven said absently, playing a video game with lots of loud explosions. “A kid's been eating your compost?”

"Nah, it's a man. But it's a little man."

"Like a midget?"

James shook his head, staring at the trapped guy, who was starting in on the loaf of bread. He didn't look upset about being trapped. "More like a gargoyle without wings."

He James put on some shoes and went out into the summer night. The trapped man was smiling, his eyes sparkling with an unearthly light.

"Who are you? Why the fuck have you been getting into my garbage?"

"I'm a magic troll," the guy said.

The next moment James was inside the cage with the food, completely naked and trapped, stale bread half-chewed in his mouth. The magic troll was outside the cage, wearing James's clothes and standing up straight. James had to crouch inside the cage. It wasn't big enough to stand up in.

"Let me out!" James grabbed the chicken-wire and shook his own quality work.

To his horror, he saw three more trolls emerge from the bushes. They grinned impishly at him, boldly making eye contact, and the four of them lifted the cage off the ground.

"Steve!" James cried out, but his roommate couldn't hear him in the house, with video games blaring. "Steve fucking help!"

They carried the cage toward the park, and the woods beyond. The one who was wearing his clothes said, "We're going to have fun."

James disappeared into the darkness.

Banana Egg Dihydroxybenzene

I was cycling to work when a banana peel descended from heaven and landed in my path. My bike-tire skidded out on the slippery yellowness and I went tumbling into the muddy ditch. I made a big splash and my hair and clothes were instantly soaked and dirty.

I wasn't angry because I'm a calm fellow and I meditate habitually. I am in a state of nearly-constant meditation. It was a lonely road and nobody saw my embarrassing spill. But I was disoriented, upside down with my hair in the ditch-stream and my feet up on the grass.

Before I had a chance to get my bearings straight I saw an object floating by in the flowing ditch-water. The object was a spotted egg, slightly bigger than my fist and bobbing and flowing with the current.

The egg focused my equilibrium and I jumped up onto my feet, scooping the egg with speed and gentleness. I nestled the precious object in my two hands.

“My daisies!” I gasped with awe. “What kind of egg is this? Where is your mother, sweet egg? Have you been abandoned? What genre of misadventure nudged you into my watery path? Oh

Lord! Grant me answers!"

But neither Zeus, Satan nor Jesus provided me with a solution to this mystery. So I took off my shirt and swaddled the exoskeletal foetus within it and abandoned my bicycle, walking home with my new egg. I decided to skip work so I could give the egg my attention. Lightning cracked in the darkening sky and the burgeoning rain-clouds looked like richly flavoured whipped-cream.

Returning to my apartment, which was a renovated suite in an old stone castle, I cast my gaze upon the infinite internet, seeking the answers which the gods denied me.

I looked up pictures of eggs to see if I could spot one that matched mine. I wanted to know which species I would be nurturing. But for all my searching I could not find anything that looked like my new friend, my little embryo. None of the internet-eggs had the perfect black circles or the smooth and creamy whiteness. I took a photo of the egg with my cell-phone and uploaded it to a forum to see if anyone would recognize it. "I'll check the forums later to see if anyone responded," I said out loud.

Then I sat the egg on my blue pillow, and it was a pretty sight indeed. Laying on my bed I beheld the beauty of this strange unborn creature. What could it be? Was it a giant bird? Was it an alligator? A dinosaur?

There were some trees behind my building,

so I gathered some fallen twigs and made a nest. I decided to keep the egg at room temperature: not knowing the species meant not knowing the ideal incubating procedure.

Over the next few days there were no useful responses to my query. Nobody knew what type of animal I was planning to hatch.

One day I saw it rocking back and forth, wiggling around. Was it about to hatch? I jumped over to the dresser-drawer where I kept its nest and I watched it. “The gods may not have granted me convenient answers, but they have granted mercy to my precious egg! Soon it will be born! I will see what kind of creature I saved from the dirty ditch!”

A section of the shell swelled and then cracked from some pressure being exerted from within. The creature was breaking out! A black thing poked through the crack, looking like a round shoulder. I knew that I should not help it break out. It had to bust into the world without assistance. A cracked split the egg in two, and a soft light glowed out from within.

“What is this light?” I asked myself. Then the shell split totally in half, revealing the baby within. It was a cell-phone, with its touch-screen glowing a soft turquoise. I picked it up in my hand. Its screen was about four inches and there were no buttons at all and no logo.

My characteristic meditative calm was seriously challenged by this unexpected electronic birth. How does a cell phone hatch from an egg?

But as I looked at the mysterious item I felt love and wonder overcoming my mental frustration. Why should I be upset that an event defied my expectations? Frustration would not help me, or the baby phone.

I cradled the baby in my hands, still revelling in its glory and not yet wondering what to do.

Then a face appeared on the screen. Or, rather, dark eyes and a smiling mouth appeared on the screen, turning the phone into a face.

The mouth opened and I felt the phone shake as it spoke through its speaker.

It said, "Hello Mother."

“War as a Machine”

Clomping up the worn wooden stairs, Colonel Gasp reflected that this old house was built for family life, not for waging war. Defying such reflections, agonized screams reached his ears from the basement. He wondered if the practitioners were busy healing the wounded, or extracting information. He heard drills, saws, and wrenching metal.

Following the scent of cigar-smoke, Gasp found the office of General Hezz. It used to be a baby's room. A carousel still hung above Hezz's desk.

Hezz himself was looking out the window. A nearby bomb-blast filled the window with cartoonish yellow light, making Hezz a blackened silhouette as he turned one-eyed and smiling to greet Gasp. He looked very comfortable in this abandoned house. He looked very comfortable as an invader in a baby's room, staring out the window at all the violence.

Gasp took a look out the window. The grim field was torn to pieces from here up to the tree-line in the distance. There were no trenches. Just a mess of violence. Robots smashing people into gore, giant hammer-fists pulverizing faces and torsoes. People wrestling, stabbing, tearing out the guts of their enemies, screaming and killing and dying. Mud and blood.

"We rise from the dirt to eat each other," Hezz said. "Like a never-ending dog-fight. There is no civilian life. Family, sports, education, just shows us that the war machine is dynamic! Everybody contributes. Don't ever doubt that you're doing what you're meant to do, Colonel Gasp."

"Just trying to do my job, sir," Gasp said. "Did you have orders for me?"

Hezz took an envelope out from his desk drawer. "Sure do, son. I need you to take this document to our base at Nuzzliscthu." He spoke slowly and clearly. "This is a very important string of information. Can I rely on you? The war effort needs this."

Gasp grabbed the document, a brown envelope with a wax seal. "How do I get there, sir?"

Hezz handed him a treasure map. Bombs exploded in the yard, illuminating the dotted line and the X-destination on the parchment. "Don't let me down, boy."

As Gasp exited the room a gang of little girls in different coloured dresses ran into the office and swarmed Hezz, eating him alive while he smoked his cigar.

Gasp clomped down the stairs and jumped out through a broken window. He landed in the dirt and hid behind a crate. A pack of dogs was killing a man in the road, tearing him to pieces when a pickup truck blasted down the lane. The vehicle smashed through the pack, crushing and scattering the animals. Gasp darted across the road after it had cleared the way, and he hopped over a picket fence, splattered with blood.

The colonel climbed a hill and lay in the dirt to get a view of what lay beyond. Now he was out of town, but he had to get across the battlefield itself. He looked at his map. He had to cross the battlefield, and then pass through the swamp to get to Nuzzliscthu.

Most of the battlefield was flat, trampled by fighting feet. But over here on the far right, there were little hills and valleys where Gasp could find cover. He crouched and stalked toward the muddy hills. Bomb blasts hid the noise of his movements. Brown clouds and smoke obliterated the sun. It was always dark here.

He made it to the hills, but a beast blocked his path. It had the face of a hawk, four arms, great wings, and it squawked a harsh warning at Gasp. Colonel Gasp pulled the pin on a grenade and hurled it at the squawker, exploding it in a mess of feathers, dirt, and guts. He stomped past its remains, and entered into the hills.

He ran past two women who were pulling out each other's hair and clawing at each other's faces, and he evaded a massive mechanical monster who was breathing fire and eating people. When a bomb flashed he saw the silhouette of two robots fighting on top of a hill, and he saw a dinosaur eating a wizard.

Climbing to the top of the next hill Gasp saw a content-looking gentleman with a mustache painting a picture. It was a landscape of a sunset over a beautiful green hill. Gasp stopped and stared in shock. He looked at the painter and said, “How can the luxury of such beauty exist in this war world?”

An army captain appeared beside the painter and pointed at the painting. Then he turned to a group of dejected-looking soldiers and said, “See this pretty picture? This is why we fight!” Then the men cheered and started stabbing each other to death. The captain shot the painter in the head, splattering brains onto his canvas. Gasp whipped out his revolver and shot six bullets into the captain’s face. Reloading, he carried on with his journey.

Descending the hill, he saw the mud turn into swamp. Dismal old trees drooped their ugly branches into the stagnant muck. Gasp shivered. It was cold. Big flies buzzed nearby.

Swamp-people emerged from the swamp, reaching out for him with their suction-tip fingers. Their whole heads were giant eyeballs, and Gasp busted each one with a bullet. Once ruptured, the giant eyes slowly deflated as thick yellow ichor oozed out. The swamp-people collapsed into the green juice, disappearing in moments.

Colonel Gasp had to struggle for each step as the swamp got thicker and deeper. Should he dare to swim? He used twine to tie the message to the top of his head, then splashed off into the water. Each stroke got thicker until he was stuck beneath a canopy of branches, getting sucked into muck. He pulled out a grenade and unwound a generous length of twine. Tying the grenade in the middle of the twine, he threw it over a thick branch. It wrapped around the branch twice and wedged in a corner.

Wrapping the twine around a fist, he pulled himself slowly out of the muck and up into the trees. His uniform was covered in green swamp juice, but the letter was safe and dry on his head.

Standing on the branch, Gasp was confronted with a bat-creature whose eyes blazed fire and whose lashing tongue was a green snake with its own red, flickering tongue. It spread its big wings and its bared teeth seemed to pulsate up and down. In the other direction there was nowhere to run. Gasp was forced to face the creature.

Dropping to a crouch and ready to spring, Gasp pulled the pin on another grenade. The monster lunged at him, reaching out with spindly arms and lashing out with its snake-tongue while it screeched. The colonel stuck his fist in the beast's mouth, penetrating the throat, where the grenade exploded.

Gasp's lower arm was incinerated, his upper arm liquefied. Bat-guts covered the swamp-guts that covered his uniform. Stumbling back and wiggling his stump, Gasp used his good hand to touch his head, verifying that the envelope was safe.

The bat's two wings were now barely stuck onto a stringy pile of raw meat. Gasp grabbed one and stretched it out. He removed his boots slowly with his left hand, then sat on the wing. He grasped one end of the wing bone with his left hand and the other with one foot, then shook himself off the branch. Controlling it with his foot and hand, he floated slowly across the swamp, avoiding a big tree and passing over two roving gangs of swamp-people. He dropped a grenade on anything that moved, always doing his part in the war effort.

The bat wing landed on the shore across the river, beside a homeless man's tent. Gasp left some money and whiskey under the old man's pillow.

Colonel Gasp travelled through a thick forest and out into a desert. The dark wind blew the sand into the shapes of humans, and the humans killed each other with sandy fists.

The wind became a dust storm and he was frightened of getting lost. But he saw a red light glowing through the gloom. He struggled against the harsh storm, sand in his bloody wound, heading toward the light.

He reached a building made of an otherworldly material, generating a steady red luminance. The building had no door. Just a mail slot. Gasp took Hezz's envelope and slid it into the slot, breathing a sigh of relief that he'd completed his mission.

Turning around to head back to the battle,

Gasp felt the ground tremble beneath him. Dust, smoke, and clouds made it difficult to see very far, but he could discern the shadowy shapes of massive creatures erupting from the earth. They were robots as large as towers, built in the shapes of beasts, and they turned to fight each other. Metal scraped across metal as the monsters roared and disfigured each other with claws and teeth. Gasp tilted his head back and laughed with joy when he saw such glory.

He saw two large and simple eyes looking down at him from a smoggy distance. The face rushed toward him, mouth gaping. As the ragged teeth clamped down on his body and took him up into the air, up into its mouth, he pulled the pin on a grenade.

Rakikomaly

Rake tumbled down the mountain. He hit the back of someone's house and smashed through their window, landing comfortably in a recliner as a man, a woman and a child watched TV.

"Who the hell are you?" said the man.

"I've just been to the top of the mountain," Rake said, "and I've seen the Grogolmonsters' horrible Keepers!"

"And did you see the Grogolmonster?" asked the little boy with fear.

"He's huge, and hideous!" said Rake, still reclining comfortably.

"Would you all be quiet?" snapped the woman. "I'm watching the news!"

Rake was wearing an anti-gravity suit and he floated out of the room. His mission hadn't been a total bust; he'd tasered the hell out of some of the Keepers and he stole a copy of the Grogoltexle, but he had been hoping to subdue the Grogolmonster.

He walked along the road to his home, which was a huge floating ball of energy. He stepped into it and it absorbed and disintegrated his body. It also recorded his brain and transferred his mind to its virtual-reality energy-computer storage. He was in a virtual- reality apartment building with a pool, a bordello, an open bar, unlimited room-service and a huge library in the basement with millions and millions of books. Heat and lights were extra.

At his virtual-reality table, virtual-reality Rake read some of the Grogoltexle. It was a bloody account of the Grogolmonsters' endless victories. But it also spoke of his weaknesses. It said that if you cut off the Grogolmonsters' tail then the monster will explode. But then the tail will turn into an immortal snake and grow to the size of a whale and eat you and terrorize the planet forever. But if you take the tail and tie it in a bunch of knots right after you cut it off then it will grow into an irreversibly-tied-up giant snake that is both useless and immortal.

This is what Rake decided to do.

The energy apartment building reconstituted Rake's body, rested, well-fed, disease-free and ready to take down the Grogolmonster.

Rake couldn't do this alone, of course. The Grogolmonsters' Keepers would have to be dealt with. So he went to the forest and sought the help of a friend, a talking unicorn whose name was Talkicorn.

Talkicorn said, "my shimmering spike shall impale many a misguided Keeper and distract them whilst you undo the Grogolmonster, but they will inevitably overcome me. We need one more warrior!"

"But whom?" Rake wondered, stroking his luxurious beard.

"I know!" said Talkicorn. "My friend the Anomaly! The Anomaly is a physical anomaly which appears to suck in any rays of light that pass near it and it spits the light back out at wrong angles and different frequencies so that the colours are changed."

"How the fuck will that help us, Talkicorn?" Rake was angry at Talkicorns' silly suggestion.

"Well the Anomaly has more powers than that," said Talkicorn. "I only mentioned its tendency to distort light because, since you and I are visually-oriented beings, that would appear to be its defining quality. In truth, all we can see is the distorted light, while the Anomaly's true nature is hidden."

"But isn't that true of all things?" said Rake, stroking his luxurious beard. "For instance, you and I can see and hear each other, but only light and sound enter our brains. Your true nature is hidden from me while I create a 3D model of your physical being inside my brain."

"Yes," said Talkicorn, "but the light and sound have been changed or created by our physical bodies, and your brain enjoys a direct connection to my physical body through those waves of sound and light. So you are at least getting a transmutation of the effects of my true nature, which can allow you to make educated guesses about my true nature."

"Then that must also be true of the Anomaly," reasoned Rake, whose luxurious beard flowed like a rich red river from his face. "You've contradicted yourself!"

"Bah!" cried Talkicorn. "These are questions we can ask the Grogolmonster after we destroy him!"

"Shouldn't we ask him these questions before we destroy him?" Rake said.

"No! He'll be trying to kill us and won't answer our questions!"

"Agreed!" said Rake, and they went to find the Anomaly.

The Anomaly was playing a cheap, dirty, single-octave electric keyboard for change outside the market. But Rake couldn't see the Anomaly. In fact, he couldn't even properly see the entrance to the market. The gate had a weird shape and there were crazy colours everywhere. Then Rake realized that this optical illusion must be the light-distorting effects of the Anomaly itself.

Talkicorn asked the Anomaly if it would join them and the Anomaly bent the light in such a way that they understood that it would dearly love to join them.

The three warriors started climbing the road up the mountain. Halfway up Rake said, "I'm getting tired. We should smoke a joint."

So they all sat down on the couch and lit a

huge joint. The Anomaly busted out some coke and they all did a couple lines. Then girls started showing up with beer and peppermint schnapps, and the party really got started.

One particularly buxom brunette sat down beside Rake and started talking to him. She said, "so, you're going to fight the Grogolmonster?"

Rake nervously swirled the ice cubes in his glass of schnapps. "Yeah," he said.

"That's so brave."

Rake blushed. "You seem really nice," he told her, putting his hand lightly on her knee.

Then a black Ford 15-seater van pulled up to the side of the road and tipped over, spilling a big wooden box out the back door. Fifteen guys dressed in black spiky armour climbed out of the van's windows, and the biggest one said, "we thought we heard a party, so we came to check it out."

"It's the Grogolmonsters' Keepers!" cried Talkicorn, forgetting about the booze and the women. "Kill them!"

"Hang on man," said the lead Keeper, "we just wanna chill."

Rake was tempted to just chill with the Keepers, because he really wanted to get to know the girl he just met. Also, every month the Keepers sacrifice one of their own to the Grogolmonster, and they always vote to see which one they want to sacrifice. That means that the least-popular (and thus least-cool) Keeper always got sacrificed, so when you meet a Keeper who's alive then they're statistically cooler than average.

"I know you guys are extra-cool," Rake said, "and it would be fun to hang out, but you're murderous and sadistic, and you nurture the evil Grogolmonster. We have no choice but to destroy you."

Rake drew his energy-sword and cut off the lead-Keeper's arms and legs in one fell swoop. Talkicorn impaled two Keepers on his spike with one thrust, then used his massive hind-legs to kick another one in the head. The Anomaly distorted light in such a way that two Keepers died. Then it distorted light in another way so that a different Keeper decided he no longer wanted to be a Keeper, and he went and started flirting with the brunette who had been talking to Rake.

Talkicorn said, "Rake! We'll take care of the Keepers, you kill the Grogolmonster!"

Rake slew his way over to the big wooden box that had fallen out of the Ford van and tore off the lid. A person-sized rabbit hopped out with big ears, a fluffy tail and dozens of gnashing mouths all over its body. Its mouths all roared deafeningly and it ate the van.

"Talkicorn!" Rake cried. "The Grogolmonster has a fluffy tail! How can we tie it in knots?"

Talkicorn was too busy to talk, so the Anomaly distorted light in such a way that Rake understood that he should cut off the

Grogolmonsters' tail first and then worry about how to tie it into knots.

Rake kicked the Grogolmonster in one of its mouths and then cut off its tail with his energy-sword. The Grogolmonsters' body exploded, but the tail was still intact. The Keepers saw this and one of them said, “well, we’ve lost. Let’s all get out of here and find some other monster to nurture.”

So Rake, Talkicorn and the Anomaly all stood around the disembodied tail wondering how to tie it into knots before it could turn into a giant immortal snake. It was already starting to slowly grow.

“Maybe if we stretch it then it will be long enough to tie into knots,” Rake said. “Here, Talkicorn bite the tail and I’ll pull on it to stretch it out.”

Talkicorn bit the tail and held it between his teeth while Rake pulled it into a long string.

“Alright Anomaly,” Rake said, “while Talkicorn and I stretch it you should distort light in such a way that the tail gets tied in a knot, okay?”

The Anomaly distorted light in such a way that Rake understood that it couldn’t tie the tail while they were both holding onto it. Then it distorted light in such a way that Rake understood that it confrontationally wanted to know whether he’d be able to tie a string if someone was holding onto each end. Then it distorted light yet again in such a way that they understood that since they had already stretched the tail they could just let go of it and then one of them could easily tie it into knots.

They let go of the tail and Rake said, "Talkicorn, you tie it into knots."

Talkicorn picked up the tail in his mouth and tried to tie it into a knot, but it wouldn't work. "You have two hands, Rake. You're the only one who can tie it in a knot."

Rake proudly tied the tail into several knots then dropped it on the ground. Then the little mass of knots grew and grew to the size of a whale, and they could all see that it was a giant green snake tied into permanent knots. The snake started crying because it couldn't move.

"Well we've defeated the Grogolmonster," said Rake. "But Talkicorn, I thought you said that the Anomaly had powers other than distorting light."

"It can also produce drugs seemingly out of nowhere," Talkicorn said. Then the Anomaly took out a film case full of green PCP paste and they all started eating it.

The Art Lover

A shard of light reflected off a glass vial in Araquadigio Anastasio's laboratory. The curve of light reminded him of the smooth swell of a woman's hips, and it inspired a sudden insight in his mind.

"A woman's body is beautiful, and also inspires desire," he said. "But why does it have to be both? Not everything beautiful is sexy, yet everything sexy is somehow beautiful. The fact that she's beautiful and the fact that she's desirable are two different things. Imagine if I was attracted to a different beautiful thing. Like a painting, or a sunrise. Wouldn't it be strange if I needed to touch and lick a well-decorated living room?"

He looked at his collection of scientific apparatus, tubes and vessels full of fluids that reminded him of reproductive organs. "Could I create such a person in my laboratory? Could I create the ultimate appreciator of art? Someone whose love of music and sculptures and paintings goes beyond the appreciation of beauty to include an insatiable sexual desire?"

This was a challenge, and the scientist went to work with a passion which itself resembled a physical need.

The detective stepped over the barricade. He felt at home in the museum. He had consciously chosen the pink suit and black tie so he would not feel like a mundane interloper in the world of art. Yet his stern, handsome face reflected the severity of his profession. “Is this a crime scene or a kid's birthday party?” He muttered to himself, looking at the confetti that covered the floor. Then realization struck his heart like a cold bath of despair. The confetti was shards of paintings.

Decorated canvas was strewn everywhere. At first he tried not to look at the goo, but he was a detective and it was his job to look at everything. So he looked at the goo.

The curator approached from among the officers, insurance agents and museum-employees. The little man was wringing his hands and frowning with worry. “Thank you for coming so quickly detective!” The curator said, giving a feeble handshake.

“This is quite a disaster,” said the detective. “Has anything been stolen?”

“At least part of every painting is accounted for, detective.” The curator spoke in a confused, desperate, whining voice. “Nothing has been stolen! It's just been... just been...”

“Ravaged,” the detective finished the other man's sentence. “These paintings have been mauled, chewed, bent, squeezed, stretched, torn, penetrated, violated, soiled, and defiled.” His tone was as grim as the look in his eyes.

The marble floors were exquisite. The decorative pillars were bold and pleasant to behold. The chandeliers were cleaned regularly, sparkling like diamonds. The walls were white granite. The ceiling red velvet. It was a beautiful scene for a horrible act of destruction. Almost a grim work of art in itself, he admitted, although he would rather have the original paintings back.

The detective paced the gallery.

There was a scrap of canvas on the floor beside the detective's expensive leather shoe. The pastel colours had been painstakingly layered onto the cloth by some obsessive artist. Destroyed forever. Stuck in a puddle of bodily fluid. Broken pieces of wooden frame lay here and there, sometimes piercing through the meticulously painted shreds of canvas, like compound fractures. The curator followed him, biting his lip and shaking his head.

The detective remembered the old days, when his younger self chose to ignore the blues while he drank a beer, giving no thought to the depths of any work of art. He'd had pictures of his family on the mantlepiece. But when he started investigating art-heists he was compelled to study the works he was paid to protect. He learned about the artists' techniques, and as he met more artists he began to learn about their motivations.

He stared into the curator's nervous face and thought to himself, *I am the true curator of these establishments. Art is an expression of the most pure parts of a human being, a gift to the world. All of life is an ever-changing work of art, and I am here to protect it all.*

“Who would do such a thing?” The curator asked.

“I have to admit,” said the detective, “as I once learned to sympathize with artists, now I begin to respect art-thieves and forgers. I appreciate their ingenuity, subtlety and taste. But those skillful crimes are different than this massacre. This is pure destruction.”

The curator gave him a funny look and the detective decided that this man had no appreciation for the works that had been destroyed. No appreciation for the dynamic depths of the human soul.

“At least there will be no trouble getting the culprit's DNA, right? He got it all over everything.”

“We'll tell you when we get the lab results,” the detective lied. This wasn't an isolated incident. It was the third art-rape this week, although this was by far the worst. They were dealing with a serial-rapist of art. The DNA would match the other two crimes, but not anything else on their files.

The curator shook his head and some of his frantic and worried energy left him. Kneeling down beside a dismembered scrap of canvas that held a fading blue sky and a dim sun, he said, “Sometimes when I see a truly beautiful painting I want to reach out and caress it. Not just the canvas or the paint though... I want the image itself in the abstract, like the form, the idea, the place or person or feeling that it represents. Maybe this monster, this art-rapist, maybe he just wants it more than me. He tears these things apart because... because he needs them and he'll stop at nothing to get them. But he can never break through the materials, and enter the essence of these works.

The detective sighed as he realized that he'd underestimated the curator's depth of character. “Tragic, maybe. But we've got to lock this guy up. He'll destroy everything we hold dear. There's a big exhibition opening next week with some of my favourite impressionist pieces. That will have to be our bait.”

Araquadigio Anastasio read the newspaper with the shame and heartbreak of a murderer's father. His creation, his son, had defiled and destroyed the things he was supposed to nourish and nurture. The scientist blamed himself. He had created the creature with such lust and ardour, and these aesthetic and historical crimes were Araquadigio's fault. He had created a monster.

There was no turning back. No way to fix the damage that had been done. But he could prevent further atrocities. He could make sure that his child never defiled another innocent painting.

He turned to his test-tubes and started to work on something new.

The impressionist exhibition was set up in the gorgeous palace of a defunct monarchy, maintained for historical and aesthetic reasons. The night before the show the paintings sat in the dark, on display and waiting for tomorrow's audience. Police officers hid in the corners while the detective watched from a perch high up on a balcony. Down below in the main ballroom were ten gorgeous pieces, their images barely visible in the dim light. A broad stairway led up to the balcony, and two hallways led to the East Wing and West Wing, each of which held more paintings.

In the detective's ear-piece one of his officers spoke to him. “Detective! I've got movement in the East Wing!”

Walking stealthily in quiet sneakers he went through a door behind him. Emerging at another balcony, he crept up to the edge and peered over onto the black and white tiled floor of the East Wing. A spotlight illuminated one massive acrylic depiction of a river valley at sunset with two nude women sunbathing by the shore. Thousands of brush strokes were visible, combining to make an entrancing scene of nature's beauty, illuminated by the fading pink sun.

A naked man stood on the floor below the giant canvas. He gazed in wonder, sporting a quivering erection.

"Should we arrest him now?" the voice spoke in the detective's ear.

"Not yet, let him make his move," he responded. He knew they could arrest the man now for trespassing, get his DNA while in lockup and easily pin him to the other crimes. But there was something about the man's gaze, the way he was looking at the landscape-mural, that made the detective curious. He wanted to see this weirdo's last moments of freedom, when he thought he was alone with the object of his affection. It was a little bit of voyeurism on the detective's part, but there were also practical reasons to observe the enemy performing his crime.

The man stepped forward, reaching out toward the painting and the detective prepared to make the call. "Wait for my word, men! Any second now we'll grab him."

The nude intruder paused. He knelt and stared up at the painting. Maybe he liked to watch for a while before... attacking.

"We've got more movement!" the voice spoke urgently in the detective's ear. "Someone's in the ballroom and they're moving toward the East Wing."

The detective's gaze jerked sharply to the door below him. He saw a second shadowy figure moving across the floor toward the nude man. Did they work in pairs? At the other sites they only found one set of DNA and one set of fingerprints. Who was this new person?

The newcomer was shrouded in shadow, but the detective could discern a feminine form. The naked man turned his head and stared at his approaching visitor. His eyes widened and his attention was riveted. He looked at her with the same wonder he had recently given the painting. His manhood was still swollen but he didn't seem embarrassed.

The visitor stepped into the light, and the detective saw that she was naked too. Her back was turned to him as she faced the naked man, and the detective saw the skin of her bare buttocks and back. But was it skin? It seemed to have the texture of canvas. She raised her hands above her head and started swinging her hips rhythmically, slowly. The naked man watched.

Her skin was many colours moving and shifting across her body. Not just colours, but painted images. A white boat sailed across blue water on her back. Flowers paraded across her ass like a liquid dream. She stepped further out into the light and her whole body was visible. She had the curves of a woman but the shape was ever-changing. Did he see three arms? Where was her face? Her hair moved around and danced with a will of its own. She turned slowly in a circle and the detective saw her canvas breasts hosting a pastel sunrise. A detailed portrait slid across her belly followed by an 18th-century cityscape. A massive acrylic oak tree meandered up her left thigh and disappeared between her legs. She threw her head back as she wiggled, thrusted, and stepped. As she danced, the detective found himself entranced by her beauty, and he wanted her more than he had ever wanted anyone before. What kind of creature was this? So lovely. He wished he could see her face but it remained hidden from his sight.

When she turned back around to face the naked man, he reached out to touch her. She did not back away. She took his hand and kissed it. His head slumped forward and the detective knew intuitively that the man was overcome with joy. The dancing woman lifted the man's hand above her head and he rose to his feet to look evenly at her face. She continued to dance, leading him out toward the exit.

In the detective's ear, one of the officers said, “They're in the ballroom. Should we arrest him now?”

“Wait,” the detective muttered, going back out onto the ballroom balcony. He didn't try to hide himself this time. He just stared down at the strange couple as they headed toward the main entrance.

“Unlock the doors,” he ordered one of his men through his mic. “Let them out.”

Now the canvas woman wasn't dancing anymore. She walked hand in hand with the man as endless colours and images rolled across her skin. Only her hair remained a constant black, but it moved around in a continuous dance.

They exited through the front doors. Running to a window, the detective watched them descend the elaborate stairs and onto the cobblestone pathway. “Let them go,” he whispered through his mic. The couple disappeared between two oak trees, and were lost in the darkness of the park.

The detective was jealous. He knew the nude man would make love to the painting-woman, and it would be unlike any experience that a normal human could understand. He wanted that woman. But he was also happy. Happy to see such anguish and appreciation find the opportunity for a healthy joy. Such joy.

Ghost Dog Writer

Lawrence sat at his computer and struggled to think of a good thesis for his essay, which was due tomorrow. The assigned topic was the impact of corporations on spirituality in the Western world, and it went way over Lawrence's head. His Belgian Shepherd dog lay on the bed and contentedly watched Lawrence stare at the blank computer screen. The breeze from the window played with the dog's shaggy fur.

"Aw man, essays suck," Lawrence mumbled. He got up and went to the kitchen to get some ketchup and crackers, plus a beer. Then he returned with his repast and slumped back in front of the computer. He dipped a cracker in the ketchup and started to put it in his mouth when his hand froze in shock.

The computer screen was full of sentences and paragraphs, even though Lawrence hadn't typed a single word. Dropping the cracker back into the ketchup bowl, Lawrence scrolled through the pages and saw that the 5000-word essay was complete!

He tried to think. "Did I actually write this essay and then forget about it?" No. That was stupid. He looked at his dog. "Xanadu! Did you write this essay?" No. That was even more stupid.

He read through the essay and found that he barely even understood it. There was no way he wrote this. It was too smart. The thesis was that corporations controlled the Earth, eliminating the awe of nature's power, thus generally eliminating spiritual feelings in the Western world of employee-slaves and addicted, brain-washed consumers. It was even fully referenced with footnotes citing works that Lawrence had never read. He spent a few minutes checking the citations, and they seemed legit.

He picked up his cell phone and called his friend Dustin. "Dustin! I think my dog wrote an essay!"

Dustin showed up a half hour later and read the essay. "Man, your dog's full of crap. Science has pushed spirituality back into the tiny details of physics and the distant reaches of space and time. But spirituality still exists. Corporations haven't destroyed it. Still, he backs up all his arguments. If you handed this in you'd probably get top marks."

Dustin crouched on the floor and looked into Xanadu's eyes. The dog thumped his tail happily and licked Dustin's face. Dustin said to him, "However, I guess that being surrounded by man-made stuff, plus being subservient to man-made power structures instead of nature, would disconnect us from the world that created us, removing our awe of the greater world and our connection to our roots. Maybe you're right, Xanadu."

Xanadu yawned heartily and rested his head on his paws, looking up at the visitor. Lawrence had no idea what Dustin was talking about.

"Let's do an experiment," Dustin said to Lawrence. "You start a story and we'll leave the room to see if the dog finishes it."

So Lawrence saved the essay to a USB card, started a new document in his word-processor and wrote, "Once upon a time..." Then they went to get some ketchup and crackers and beer, leaving Xanadu alone with the computer.

When they returned the page was once again filled with text. Dustin checked the word count. "It's two-hundred and forty-thousand words! The dog wrote a fucking novel!"

Xanadu was lazing on the bed, nonchalant and carefree. Half-asleep.

Lawrence also handed in his essay and got an A. They printed off the novel and Dustin spent the weekend reading it. It was a sweeping epic about a group of warriors pledged to protect an alien artifact which documents the origins of life on Earth. Throughout the centuries the warriors died and were replaced by new recruits, each with their own obstacles and enemies to face. Their common link was a shared recurring dream-theme, where the human-like aliens communicated with the warriors and tried to guess at which point humanity would be ready to read the artifact.

Dustin met Lawrence at Lawrence's basement-apartment and dropped the heavy manuscript on his kitchen table. “This book is awesome,” he said.

“I got an A for that essay,” Lawrence said glumly. “I'm scared. Where did the essay come from?”

Dustin waved his hand to dismiss his friend's concern. “Don't worry about how it happened. This is a goldmine! You should try to publish this book!”

Xanadu walked in, his claws clicking on the ceramic tile. He went up to Dustin so the guest could pat his shaggy head, then the dog sat down comfortably on the floor.

“What an awesome dog,” Dustin said with a smile.

Lawrence frowned. “I don't like books. And this scares me. I didn't even want to come to university. My mom said I have to, but I can just work at Dad's store. University is for girls and nerds.”

Dustin's eyes were a million times brighter than Lawrence's, and he clutched his dull friend's shoulder and squeezed. “You can make a lot of money from this stuff, man! And pay the dog back by buying him good biscuits! If we do this right we can buy a big house with a gigantic back yard for Xanadu to run around in. We'll buy him some girl-dogs to fool around with. He'll be a stud."

Lawrence was no match for his zealous friend's enthusiasm and intelligence, so he agreed with the plan and together they wrote a cover-letter and sent the book to a small publisher. Within a few weeks they got a response. The book had been accepted.

By the time the book got accepted they had already produced five more novels, each one more epic than the last.

One of the novels was a far-future, post-humanism piece of science-fiction. After reading it Dustin shook his head and said, "Man, how does this dog have so much knowledge? And such diverse interests? And how does he write a whole book in like two minutes?"

This was the first time that the situation started to become uncomfortable for him. In his excitement he had ignored the mysterious implications of such a phenomenon, but now the questions were starting to sink in. *How was this happening? Was it really Xanadu's doing? What were the possible negative repercussions?*

Also, this science-fiction story was incredibly violent... almost sadistically violent. It was so violent that Dustin felt guilty as he sent the manuscript to an agent. But when he held their first royalty-checks in his hand he found that his greed overcame his disquiet. They gave the dog partial credit by publishing under the pen-name, "Xanadu Xavier."

They got an agent and got signed on with a big publishing company. Xanadu was so prolific that Lawrence and Dustin each had to pretend to be separate authors, and they each published under two pen-names, with Xanadu Xavier as the main one.

The themes of Xanadu's books varied wildly, but the guys noticed a strange trend. The dog was leaning more and more into psychologically disturbing themes, with lots of violence.

One book was about a family of serial killers. When the mother and father were killed by one of their intended victims, the young children kept up the habit by killing lots of other people, including their school-mates.

Another book was about the entire world being driven insane by recurring rape-nightmares.

Dustin was sitting on Lawrence's floor, finishing a manuscript entitled, "Jesus Nightmare." Xanadu was sleeping on the floor beside him. Jesus Nightmare was about a little boy who went to Sunday School and then Jesus visited him in a dream. At first Jesus was very kind, but the book described the saviour as a scrawny, twitching, decrepit malingerer who looked like a drug addict. At first Jesus only visited the boy in his dreams and told him nice things, but he slowly started filling the kid's mind with fear and doubt and guilt. Then he started showing up in real life when nobody was around. And he would play around with time, making the boy relive the same day over and over, or sending him into the future by a few days. The boy grew into a neurotic, anti-social mess. His parents got angry and very scared at their child's behaviour, but Jesus smiled sweetly, caressed the boy's cheek and said, “They don't love you. They're not real. Only I am real. I am the word and I am the world.” Throughout the course of the story, Jesus made it clear to the boy that there is no separation between God and Satan... in fact there is just Satan's mind and nothing else, and the supposed love of Jesus is just the sweet bait and seduction for psychological torture. The whole world was made by Satan to torment and torture people... but even those people, those victims were just figments of Satan's mind, created to be tortured by the ultimate sado-masochist creator. The world was masochistic solipsism incarnate. The book ended with the poor boy crying and falling deeper into a bottomless pit of metaphysical fear and insanity.

Dustin put the book down and took a deep breath. Xanadu looked up at him with interested eyes, wagging his tail. “Jesus Christ, Xanadu. What's wrong with you?”

Lawrence stopped reading the stories. He finally told Dustin, in a shaking voice, “You can keep all the money. I don't like this. I don't want to do this.” He had become increasingly depressed for three reasons: 1) His own inability to appreciate the richly imaginative and insightful prose; 2) the increasingly violent, disturbing and generally malevolent stories, and; 3) the fact that a dog was apparently writing the stories.

Jesus Nightmare became a bestseller, which made Dustin shake his head at the gory nature of human taste and curiosity. Eventually it became too much even for him, and he stopped getting the dog to write new stories. He felt like he was messing with a force that he did not understand, and he might have bit off more than he could chew. Still, he kept collecting the royalty-checks (putting half aside for Lawrence, just in case his friend changed his mind and wanted his half). He didn't see much of Lawrence lately. He wasn't going to any of his classes, and Dustin stopped visiting his apartment.

One day Dustin was drinking some expensive scotch, purchased with the royalties of Jesus Nightmare, when his cellphone beeped to indicate that he had new email. Opening the email app, he saw that the email was from Lawrence. It was a suicide-note.

“Dustin, you can keep all the royalties. I can't do this anymore. This is more than irresponsible. This is like evil magic and I think we did something really bad to the planet. I'll spend the rest of my life worrying about it, so I'm just ending it now. Goodbye. Sorry.”

Dustin's eyes grew wide with fright and he rushed to his bike, fast pedal-pumping to his friend's apartment.

The front door was locked, so Dustin

screamed and kicked it repeatedly until the lock broke. The kitchen was empty, and he ran into Laurence's room. The scene was horrible. Lawrence was decapitated with his body bleeding out on his bed. His head rested on the floor, dumb eyes staring up at nothing. There was blood everywhere. Blood on the white sheets, the gray carpet, and splattered on the thin curtains which blew peacefully in the wind from the open window. Xanadu was sitting up and looking at Dustin, thumping his tail happily.

The computer screen was on. Laurence's email was open. Dustin read the email. It was a confession email, labelled from Dustin's account to the police. It said, "I made a big mistake. I wanted all the royalties from our books because I did most of the work, but he wouldn't let me have it so I killed him. I thought I could get away with it but now I feel sick. I don't know what to do. The books are really violent and it made us both feel weird. Now I've killed my friend. I cut off his head. Please help. I'll wait here at Laurence's house. Love, Dustin McCarthy."

The email had already been sent to the police.

Dustin looked at Xanadu, who thumped his tail happily on the floor. "Xanadu! Did you send this? You sent the suicide-email to me too, to lure me here! Why? Why, Xanadu? We were going to buy you a big house with a back yard!"

The sound of sirens drifted through the

window.

When the cops came in Dustin tried to explain, very calmly. “It was the dog. He sent the email. He killed Laurence. He wrote all the books. *You've got to believe me.*”

Later on his lawyer explained the forensics results. “The suicide-email that you got on your phone was sent after Laurence died. He didn't send it. There were no fingerprints on the murder weapon, but your prints are all over the keyboard and all over the house. It wasn't a suicide, since he's completely decapitated. It was clearly a murder and you're the only suspect. It doesn't look good.”

Dustin insisted on pleading not-guilty, and he insisted on blaming the dog.

He was declared unfit to stand trial and sent to an asylum indefinitely.

Through newspapers Dustin learned that Xanadu was sold at a police auction. A physicist bought him. It wasn't long before that physicist became famous for a series of groundbreaking discoveries in theoretical physics. Dustin tried very reasonably to explain to his doctor that he needed to get in touch with the physicist, to warn him about Xanadu. His request was denied. The doctors stopped allowing Dustin to read the newspaper. So Dustin never had to find out about all the military uses of the new scientific discoveries.

113

Demon Numbers

“Izzn shig nakwanay,” the security guard greeted Nick and Lindsay as they stepped into the lobby.

Nick stopped short. “What did you say, Dan?”

The security guard's smile disappeared. “Rae scald lodden shig.”

Nick shared a confused look with Lindsay. Then Dan's walkie-talkie squawked some noise and he put it to his face and said, “Dan here,” before turning away to converse with the caller.

The receptionist waved as they walked past.

On the elevator Lindsay said, “That was weird wasn't it? That guy?”

“Dan? Yeah he wasn't making any sense. But then he talked fine on the walkie-talkie.”

“I'm excited to see your equipment. You talked about it so much I had to visit.”

Nick said, “It's boring, now that it's all running. Setting it up was the fun part.”

She said, “I'm used to taking care of myself. I think it's that same instinct that makes me need to see where your money comes from, with my own two eyes.”

"At least you admit you're a control freak."

"Just humour me, *honey*." She slapped his ass.

The doors opened and Nick led the way down the hall. "Well the money's coming just in time," he said. "You'll have to go on maternity in a few months, and you'll have to hire a manager to take care of the restaurant. Giving up even more control!"

His keys jangled as he swung the door inwards, fumbling on the left for the lights. It was a tiny office, jam packed with equipment but neatly organized. Stepping in, he gestured at one wall, which was stacked with layer upon layer of identical rack-mounted computers. "These are the expensive ones," he told her, unable to hide his pride. "They're linked together into a miniature supercomputer. A lot faster than the old setup, although we still keep the old stuff running over here." He pointed at the opposite wall, with a few dozen desktop computer towers lined up on layers of metal shelving. They were all different models, bought second-hand and rebuilt for Nick's purposes. The annoying hum and blinking lights indicated ongoing activity.

Lindsay said, "You really need all this equipment just to... decipher codes?"

He nodded. "I'm providing huge processing power. We download encrypted code, decipher it with a decryption key they gave us, then upload the decrypted code to another guy, the compiler.

Everything is anonymous."

"Including the guy who pays you.."

"They use Paypal. I'm comfortable with not asking questions. I'm not doing anything illegal and I don't want to burn this contact. Plus, the equipment has already paid for itself. We're beyond the point of risk. It's just easy money now."

"Why doesn't the client just buy this equipment and solve the codes himself?"

"Too much work for one person. I receive a constant stream of new code through multiple internet connections, constantly running on all this hardware, but I'm just one solver. There are other solvers, and then we upload the code to compilers who put the codes together into bigger ones. That's pretty much all I know. They're basically just renting my processing power... at a generous price."

"I never liked the secrecy, but I trust you. Thank you for bringing me to see it."

He kissed her cheek. "I wanted to show it off anyway."

She squeezed his hand and said, "Nuy blit shoonig."

"What?"

"I didn't say anything," she said. "Did I?"

----- ----- -----

Cheap computer speakers blared an alarm, waking Harrison from another uncomfortable sleep. With bleary eyes and a clumsy hand he fumbled for his glasses, which were on a milk-crate beside his cot. He accidentally knocked his Bible to the floor and spilled a cup of water on it before grasping his spectacles and putting them on.

Harrison grumbled, sat up straight, and picked up the book. Too late. The pages were already damp. He threw his blanket on the carpet to soak up the rest of spill, patting it down. Wasted effort. The polyester blanket wasn't very absorbent.

The alarm was still buzzing. A block was finished. He ran a hand through his long, greasy hair, stepping barefoot across the cold basement room he was renting. Harrison logged into his computer to check out the alarm. He smiled with excitement when he saw the message: “Block 627 Successfully Compiled.”

“That's why they call me the compiler,” he muttered proudly to himself as he sat down. He looked at a second screen and saw that Block 628 was 80% finished too. “Just a few more pieces from the solvers and I can start compiling Block 629.”

With the alarm off he could hear the beautiful hum of all these computers. He loved that hum. He actually made audio recordings of it so he could listen to it on headphones when he left the office. He felt like there was a message in that hum. That's why he slept here in the office while the codes were compiling, so he could absorb it in his sleep.

Of course he couldn't tell anybody about that message. Not with his history. For now it had to be his own personal, private message. He glanced at his drying Bible and knew that somehow there was a connection. Data streams.

Harrison folded the cot back up into a chair, pulled out his pipe and a bag of weed from a drawer, then sat back with his Bible to smoke a bowl and listen to the hum. The smoke seemed to hum as harshly in his lungs as the computers did in his ears. Secret Knowledge. That's what he wanted. But it was, by definition, hard to find.

As he lay back and relaxed, the hum seemed to form shapes in his mind. He could hear garbled human voices speaking nonsense to him from the computers, where Block 28 was running all its decrypted solutions through its processors. Part of the hum was from the cooling fan and other parts of the multiple computers, but the processors were whining their own backup music. Sometimes he had to struggle to hear it, but once he found it he started to hear the voice and its incomprehensible message.

He listened to the voice, searching for some meaning. "Hibe rae izzn valem bit yim braken folt godden baze..." He wanted someone else to listen, to tell him if they could hear it too. But he couldn't risk it. He'd made that mistake before.

"Kasten sub narco natwanay shig..."

Who were the solvers who sent these decrypted messages?

Who was the contact, with the ever-changing email address, to whom Harrison sent the compiled blocks?

"Zade hetmasten groo..."

The voice was almost monotone, like a chant from an electronic demon. Whenever the pitch did change it would strike odd notes, not following the melodic patterns of human speech to convey human emotion. It was something foreign and inhuman.

He put a finger on the gold-print crucifix embedded on the front of his damp book, thinking of the history of this particular relic of information. Like any book, the Bible was just a long string of characters. A data stream which deeply affects the minds of those who run it through the processor of their brains.

"Seig druff snime groo rull..." the voice spoke, droning on in Harrison's ears. He wondered if he could memorize it like a chant. If he could repeat it. That seemed like the natural thing to do. To open himself up to this voice and make it a part of him. To take a piece of it into his mind, into the network of his brain.

He grabbed his handheld digital recorder and went over to the computer, now processing Block 628. Pulling a latch, he opened the side of the computer tower and laid the panel against the next unit. Now the voice came through unfiltered. He adjusted the equalizer on his recorder to pick up more of the processor's higher-pitched drone, and he set the recorder next to the motherboard.

Then he sat back and listened.

----- ----- -----

As the glass door swooshed shut behind him, Nick noticed Dan wasn't here today. There was a different security guard instead. A handsome woman who nodded politely.

Nick went to the reception desk. “Hi Cheryl. Dan sick?”

Cheryl beckoned him close, “Dan was arrested.”

“Arrested for what?”

She whispered, “killing his son.”

“You're joking.”

She beckoned him close again. “He burned him alive! My boss told me.”

“She's playing a joke with you.”

Cheryl shook her head.

Nick didn't believe it. There was something wrong here. He recalled Dan talking funny yesterday.

When he went up to his office some of his lines of code were solved and ready to be sent to the compiler. Now he could download more codes and collect some money. He had to use FTP to upload the finished files onto the compiler's server. He went to his desktop screen to open the FTP program, but he noticed a strange file in the middle of his desktop. It was a text file entitled,

"DangerousGibberish-README.txt" The file wasn't there before. He hadn't created it and he didn't recognize it.

Letting his cursor hover over the file, it took him a moment to collect his thoughts. Where did this file come from? Invasive software? Hackers? Maybe a physical break-in?

He didn't open it. Instead, he got up and looked around for signs of a break-in. He checked the lock on his door, the vents, the window. They all looked fine, all secured from the inside.

Normally he would get in touch with his contact about an issue like this. But those words, "Dangerous gibberish," suddenly held a lot of meaning for him. Because of Dan. Because of Lindsay. Curiosity overtook him.

He rummaged through his desk drawer and found an old android tablet. Plugged in the USB and transferred the file. He took out the SIM card and turned off the wi-fi, then opened the file on the quarantined device.

He half-expected his tablet to crash from a hidden virus. But it simply opened his word-processor, displaying a confusing message:

"Imagine a dark star programmed to pump out particle streams in a pulsing rhythm that carried a message. Imagine if these dark particles had mass, but passed right through our world and our bodies like light passes through glass.

Picture the right kind of crystal, in the right kind of environment, with the right kind of equipment, to record fluctuations in the crystal matrix as these ghost particles of invisible matter passes through it, interacting weakly.

Imagine millennia of wise men recording and deciphering these messages from ancient outer space. Recording them in chants and texts. Using other sources of knowledge to develop a decryption key so we can finally transpose this data stream into something meaningful.

Imagine if someone sent the decryption key to you, and fed you the data stream to decipher. And as you ran the code through your processor it created a magnetic field and an audible sonic vibration which interacted with your brain and rearranged the patterns and connections of your mind. The mind of Dan. The mind of your wife. Imagine if it changed you.

What if you crossed the threshold without knowing it? Now data streams (creatures) stored in dark matter could finally interact with the living world. You have given them life.

Think about your own mind, consisting merely of matter and energy arranged in a certain pattern. Such power in patterns. Such potential.

Imagine becoming a gateway and an ally, sharing in this new power which you helped bring to Earth. Money and power. Secrets.

Or walk away and eventually be consumed.

Izzn hi gloon bastok."

Nick stared at the screen, at the blinking cursor, and tried to rationalize this message. At first he wasn't scared, just focused on the elements of this mystery, trying to connect them into something he could understand.

"This is a joke," he said again, but hew knew it wasn't. Dan's gibberish had caught Nick's attention right away, and now Dan had killed his son. Burned his son alive. This message mentioned Dan, mentioned the gibberish... mentioned *his wife*. Fear crept into Nick's heart.

Suddenly he became very aware of the noises his computers were making, and the room felt hot and dry. Mostly he just heard the cooling fans, but there were other noises too. Clicking, whining... it was all drowned out by the fans. But now...

"Hin ziz nan toog..."

Nick shook his head, frightened because he could hear a voice somewhere in the computer-noises. He couldn't think. He couldn't process this.

He listened closer, needing to discover that the voice was imaginary.

"Griss roo tolt fill..." The kinds of words Dan and Lindsay had said.

It was almost monotone, the pitch shifting occasionally to create a disturbing alien melody. Nick wanted it out of his mind. Out of his life. He kept listening, hoping it would go away. But it continued, so obvious now that he was surprised he hadn't noticed before.

Had he lost his mind? Was this how schizophrenia started? Except that Dan was really in jail, talking the same gibberish, replaced at work by a new woman. Lindsay had heard it too. She'd spoken it without even realizing it. Here in this room. His family.

The obvious thing to do was to get rid of all this equipment. No more processing strange codes, no more incomprehensible babbling, no more sons burned alive... *no more money.* It seemed so drastic. He'd look crazy when he told Lindsay he was scrapping the equipment because of space-ghosts. There couldn't really be any harm in this software, could there?

"I need someone to talk to," he said. But nobody would understand. Who else knew about this stuff? The anonymous person or persons who sent him the codes must have some answers. But could he trust them? He had no access to other solvers.

Suddenly it came to him. *The compiler!* He

needed to get in touch with the compiler. The compiler put all the finished codes together. So maybe he was experiencing similar stuff. Maybe he had similar fears, and some insight.

Nick wrote his own text file on his PC. Then he uploaded the file to the compiler's server using FTP.

----- ----- -----

Harrison sat in a busy coffee shop on Dundas Street. He couldn't hear the clink and chatter of mugs and conversation, because his headphones drowned out the noise. This recording was one hour long, and he'd mostly memorized it. Leaning over and staring down at his coffee, he muttered the words to himself as they spoke inside his ears. He had hundreds of hours of recordings. But he had to focus on this particular one-hour track as practise so he could learn to memorize longer pieces. He fantasized about leaving the city and becoming a monk with no distractions to keep him from this chant. This data stream.

A man sat down across from him, and it must be Nick the Solver, wearing the agreed-upon Blue Jays hat for easy identification.

“Hi,” Nick said. Harrison glanced up for a second but didn't return the greeting. Nick looked nervous, holding his cup of coffee tight with both hands.

“Are you...” Nick trailed off.

"Yeah," Harrison said, and his voice was cracked and strained. The word didn't come out right at first, just a squeak and a wheeze because he hadn't spoken to anyone in days, except to buy food and coffee. He cleared his throat. "Yeah, we exchanged some files," Harrison said, not giving his name or too much information.

"I'm Nick. Thanks for meeting me. Lucky we're both in Toronto."

Harrison shrugged and grudgingly pulled both headphones out of his ears, instantly missing the voice. "Somebody organized this project. Maybe they wanted people in the same city. Don't know why but probably not luck."

"I think it might be Dangerous," Nick said seriously, leaning in and whispering with wide eyes. He had no sense of style. Clearly upset, everything was coming with undignified interest and honesty. "Did you get the same text file as me?"

That text file, which Nick mentioned in the file he sent Harrison, was the only reason Harrison agreed to meet him. In fact, he felt a little jealous. "I had to figure this stuff out for myself," Harrison said. "Nobody sent me any messages. What did yours say?"

Nick pulled a folded piece of paper out of his pocket and handed it to Harrison. "I printed it out."

As Harrison read it a smile stretched across his face. This confirmed all his beliefs. Suddenly he was less alone.

A moment ago he felt paranoid, but Harrison was suddenly tingling with excitement. “The sun's harsh rays give us power,” he said, looking right into Nick's frightened eyes. “Like radiating codes to organize the wet Earth into human life and consciousness. Are our codes being sent from a dark sun? Or some ancient alien race?”

From the look on Nick's face, Harrison could see that the solver didn't share his enthusiasm. Harrison didn't care. “Imagine if the universe was designed with built-in passwords to tap into new regions of existence and experience, just waiting for us to find them. Not from aliens, but from gods. We could access metaphysical information, patterns for the kind of power we think of as magical. Prophecy and telekinesis, all attainable through data streams. I'm trying to learn them. You can learn, too.”

Nick slowly shook his head. No way for Harrison to tell what the solver was thinking, but easy to see what he was feeling. Fear and confusion. Nick said, “I have a wife. She's pregnant. I need to get away from this, but the letter said...”

Harrison re-read that part out loud. “Walk away and eventually be consumed.” He didn't care. “You got into this for money, and now you're scared because you found something bigger. I saw a greater power than money. Now we have it in our hands. And it's burning you. Burning you because you're scared. You need to embrace it.”

Nick turned and walked out the door, knocking his chair over in his frightened hurry. Putting his headphones back in, Harrison pressed play and started chanting along with the gibberish.

----- ----- -----

Heading back to the office, all that Nick could think about was fire. Fire to burn Dan's son alive. Cleansing fire to disrupt the ongoing data stream of Dan's offspring. The pattern of his mind, now disrupted. It was Nick's fault that Dan was a murderer.

Fire to destroy. Nick could unplug all the internet connections, but the solved code still lived inert inside the hard drive. He could delete it, but he knew that pressing the delete key doesn't necessarily physically erase anything. But fire, fire could erase it. Scramble it into oblivion.

He blew past the new security guard, emotionally unable to acknowledge her. Cheryl said, "Hi Nick."

Nick said, "Shunak tikia shig."

Then, upstairs in the office, unplugging cables and disconnecting power. Dissembling computers and pulling out hard drives. A screwdriver, a hammer, a knife, paper and matches. Electronic guts everywhere. Fire in the waste basket, toss in the dismantled hard disk. Break the motherboard in half, roast the processor like a futuristic marshmallow. The sprinklers come on, hissing like a snake, trying to heal the burning evil, so Nick moves the fire under his desk.

His thoughts become increasingly blurry. Police and fire department. He tries to talk but nobody understands. Handcuffs but everybody is very kind. Cheryl explains that Nick was stressed out because of Dan. Thank God nobody was hurt. They'll probably press charges but he won't go to jail. Doesn't matter either way. He destroyed it. He walked away. Lindsay is safe.

----- ----- -----

A Chinese doctor rubbed coupling gel on Lindsay's swelling belly for the twelve week ultrasound. Nick held her hand while they waited for the image. He owed a lot of money for the damage the fire did to his rented office, and his income source was trashed, but he'd avoided a criminal record. Plus, he hadn't heard anybody speaking gibberish since he'd burned his equipment.

The baby appeared on the screen in black and white with its big bulbous head and cute little arms. Nick felt Lindsay's hand tighten around his, so he squeezed back and took a look at her proud, smiling face. “Beautiful,” she breathed.

“Hmm, that's strange,” the doctor said.

“What?” Lindsay said with a hint of worry.

Nick saw what the doctor was talking about. He saw the wriggling legs. Too many legs, writhing and shifting bonelessly.

"They look like tentacles," Nick muttered, leaning forward and peering at the screen.

Lindsay looked deflated, pale. "Dreams," she gasped. "I dreamed about things with tentacles."

Nick looked up at the doctor. "Have you ever seen something like this before? Is this okay?"

The doctor said, "Izzn nesk trant shig kroo..."

About the Author:

Matt Payne lives in Canada.

28339720R00077

Printed in Great Britain
by Amazon